Gracie Adams actually felt sorry for Dr. Hart.

She'd always been outrageously outgoing by nature, and she'd grown up in Safe Harbor, after all, with its strange traditions and irascible characters. It was all she'd ever known, and she was perfectly comfortable in this uncommon little part of the world.

But Kyle Hart was different. He came from another world entirely. He was educated, distinguished, refined. He wasn't some hick right off the farm who looked at the bachelor's block as his opportunity to make his mark in the world.

Her heart swelled into her throat. Gracie knew how much it was costing Kyle now not to jump right off that block and make a run for it.

The next moment, her decision was made and her heart was firm.

"One thousand dollars," she said, her voice as crystal clear as her mind was made up, and as her heart was strong and true.

"The doctor has been sold. To me."

Books by Deb Kastner

Love Inspired

A Holiday Prayer #46
Daddy's Home #55
Black Hills Bride #90
The Forgiving Heart #113
A Daddy at Heart #140
A Perfect Match #164
The Christmas Groom #195
Hart's Harbor #210

DEB KASTNER

is the wife of a Reformed Episcopal minister, so it was natural for her to find her niche in the Christian/inspirational romance market. She enjoys tackling the issues of faith and trust within the context of a romance. Her characters range from upbeat and humorous to (her favorite) dark and brooding heroes. Her plots fall anywhere between, from a playful romp to the deeply emotional.

When she's not writing, she enjoys spending time with her husband and three girls and, whenever she can manage, attending regional dinner theater and Broadway musicals that tour her area.

HART'S HARBOR

DEB KASTNER

Love Inspired.

Published by Steeple Hill Books™

Special thanks and acknowledgment
are given to Deb Kastner for her contribution
to the SAFE HARBOR series.

STEEPLE HILL BOOKS

ISBN 0-373-87217-8

HART'S HARBOR

Copyright © 2003 by Steeple Hill Books, Fribourg, Switzerland

Visit us at www.steeplehill.com

Printed in U.S.A.

Let me take refuge in the shelter of Thy wings....
—*Psalms* 61:4

To Mom and Dad—
for sacrificing your own good pleasure so that
my family might have a Safe Harbor of our own.

May your love shown to us come back
to you a hundredfold.

Chapter One

❧

"**D**r. Hart! Wait up!"

Dr. Kyle Hart whirled on his heels and stuffed his hands into the pockets of his white lab coat, automatically searching for one of the apple-flavored candies he'd placed there earlier. Closing his fingers around a candy, he quickly and one-handedly unwrapped it and popped it into his mouth, while his other hand automatically brushed back through his thick black hair.

His flame-haired, emerald-eyed, swift-smiling and enchantingly gregarious nurse, Gracie Adams, was heading his direction, patently limping on her high-heeled pumps and waving a clipboard over her head, papers flapping and pencils flying everywhere.

Kyle pursed his lips, trying to hide his amusement, though he knew it must show from his eyes.

A person would think, looking at Gracie, that she was in the direst need of his assistance.

He highly doubted it. In the small, cozy town of Safe Harbor, Wisconsin, very little rated of truly *direst* need. Gracie Adams just happened to be one of those women for whom everything was an emergency.

He smiled as she approached, and gestured lightly in the direction of her clipboard. "What is it this time, Gracie?"

She looked him straight in the eye, which surprisingly wasn't hard for her to do. At six feet two inches tall, Kyle towered over most women and a good many men; but Gracie was tall and lithe, a natural-born model if ever there was one.

New York would love her.

Gracie ought to *be* a fancy New York runway model, now that he thought about it. She would be a raging success in the city with that hair and that figure.

But Kyle would never be the one to suggest such a thing to her. Gracie possessed a sweet, small-town charm he wouldn't want to see her lose, much less be the one who pointed her in that direction.

Kyle knew firsthand how dark a big city could feel, what being around a profusion of cynical people could do to a man.

Or a woman.

He wouldn't wish it on his worst enemy, and definitely not on a small-town sweetheart like the lovely and spirited Gracie Adams.

Kyle smiled at her, and Gracie returned his grin with one of her own contagious smiles. Her expression, however, remained just a little bit suspicious, from Kyle's perspective. He wondered what she had to be suspicious about.

"What do you need?" he asked again, wondering if he really wanted to hear the answer, and deciding that, whatever the risk, he did want to know what was going on in that pretty head of hers, though he might live to regret it in the long run. "What is it you need me to do for you, Gracie?"

"I think we ought to run off together."

Kyle's jaw dropped, and for a moment he did nothing but stare at her, stunned immobile from the top of his head to the tips of his cowboy-booted feet. Even his tongue refused to work, though he tried frantically in that one moment to make a witty comeback. Or at least to say something. Anything.

The moment seemed a lifetime to Kyle, but he knew in reality it had only actually only been the space of a breath. He blinked hard and recovered nearly as fast as he'd frozen, straightening and looking her right in the eye with a wink.

Gracie was obviously trying to unsettle him. Which, he admitted wryly, and only to himself, she had done quite successfully. For that one small moment in time, he'd almost believed her.

Almost.

Not that he was going to give her the satisfaction of knowing she'd yanked the proverbial rug from under him. He had his pride.

"Where do you want to run to?" he asked cryptically. "Paris? London? A tropical island in the Bahamas, perhaps?"

She groaned and shook her head fervently, waving him away with the open palm of her free hand. "Anywhere, as long as it's not here."

He chuckled at her candor. "And what is wrong with *here?*"

"Mmm. Yes, well, let's just say I want to see the big, wide world before I settle down to small-town insignificance."

Her tone was teasing, but Kyle sensed the truth behind her words. He reached out an arm and grasped her elbow, half to guide her down the hall, and half to reassure her she wasn't alone. He took her clipboard and tossed it on a nearby counter. "Believe me, Gracie, you're not missing anything. Safe Harbor is as good as it gets."

She looked at him, her gaze wide, and her full lips turned down with just enough stubbornness to hint of a pout. "Don't be discouraging."

"Well, it's true. And you're avoiding my question. What's wrong with *here,* anyway?"

Gracie just stared back at him without answering, her sparkling eyes full of the thoughts she refused to speak aloud.

He stopped and turned in front of her, forcing her to look up at him. "Gracie, why do you want to run away from home?"

The silence was deafening, at least from Kyle's point of view. He made it a rule to stay out of others' personal lives, and the one time he'd made an exception, he'd managed to stun his usually chatter-friendly nurse into complete silence.

"I'm afraid I can't do Paris this afternoon," he added when she continued to stare at him as if he'd grown a second nose. "I have patients scheduled for this afternoon, and I wouldn't want to let them down. I'm sure you have patients of your own to attend to. But we can do lunch if you'd like."

"Lunch?" She still looked dazed, but at least he had her talking.

"Sure. You know, a little food, a cup of strong, hot coffee…we can set every tongue at the Women's League wagging without even leaving town. Stir up a little gossip, you know?"

She arched an eyebrow, and he chuckled softly at his own joke. "What do you say? Does that sound good to you or not?"

He turned to her side, put a hand to the small of her back and gestured her to the right, down another hallway that led to the rear entrance to the building. He didn't really want any tongues wagging—not with his name attached to them, anyway. He was staying here in Safe Harbor to lay low for a while, not to become a public spectacle ripe for town gossip.

But for some unexplained reason, he felt obligated to Gracie Adams. Somewhere within the conversation, he had become personally committed to getting that beaming smile back on her lovely face, even at the expense of his own anonymity.

As if summoned by his reflection, her smile returned, illuminating her face like the lighthouse at the end of town. "It has potential."

"What has potential? The wagging tongues, or the food?"

She pursed her lips, then answered decisively. "Food."

He chuckled and shook his head. "So what are you in the mood for? What sounds good to you? The Bistro or Harry's Kitchen?"

He realized as soon as he asked the question how obvious, almost foolish, it sounded. The Bistro was clearly the type of restaurant tantamount to Gracie's unique style and personality. A real gentleman would not have hesitated. He'd simply have taken her to the classy joint.

"Harry's," she said immediately, to Kyle's surprise. She tugged on his arm so he would face her. "And I'm buying."

His pride welled up in quick defense. "I was the one who suggested it, Gracie. I'm buying," he retorted in a vain attempt to salvage what was left of his injured male dignity.

Gracie snorted a laugh and took his arm, pulling him down the hallway. What annoyed him most was that he let her do it.

"Don't be stubborn, Hart. I'm going to buy you lunch, and you're going to let me." The pixieish smile she flashed him let him know without a doubt she'd won this battle.

And she knew it.

"Do you always get what you want?" he asked, holding the door for her as they exited the Safe Harbor Family Practice building where they'd both spent a busy morning helping patients. The sun was shining brightly, and they both donned their sunglasses as they walked.

Gracie shrugged, appearing not to take the least offense at his less than innocent question. "Oh, pretty much."

She paused and met his gaze, her smile fading into a playful pout that left him wondering what she was really thinking. "Except when it really counts."

"Leaving Safe Harbor," he supplied for her, taking a stab in the dark.

She nodded.

Kyle wondered not for the first time why Gracie was so intent on leaving such a charming small town. The town she'd been born and raised in.

He was certainly glad to be in Safe Harbor, and he was especially glad Gracie was here now, with him. Apart from his friends Robert and Wendy McGuire, who'd been fundamental in bringing him to Safe Harbor a couple of months ago, Gracie was one of the few people here with whom he felt genuinely comfortable talking, at least beyond exchanging simple, civil niceties.

She was brutally honest, but he found he liked that in a woman—or at least, *this* woman.

Besides, she was a real trip to be around. He never knew what to expect with her. Never knew what she would say or do. In his staid and somewhat stoic life, she was a refreshing breath of air.

He'd never before been in as intimate a situation with her as this lunch situation proposed, but she was a close friend of the McGuires and had been introduced to him early on in his stay at Safe Harbor as someone he particularly ought to get to know. Perhaps there had even been a certain suggestive gleam in his old friend Robert's eyes. And since she also worked in the clinic with him, he'd had ample opportunity to get to know her.

At least superficially.

This was the first time she'd shared any information of any real depth with him, though she was certainly friendly enough in offering cursory details of her life. He'd always known there was more to her than she was letting on, layers she was merely hinting at in her conversation.

But whatever she had tucked away in that pretty head of hers had remained that way, and he'd respected that privacy up until now.

He had his own secrets to keep, too.

But now, he'd accidentally scratched beneath the surface of Gracie's because of the guess he'd made about her desire to leave Safe Harbor. Which was, he mused uneasily, nothing more than conjecture for him.

Who would have known a man like him, who preferred a medical manual to any kind of emotion whatsoever, would be able to come remotely close to—never mind actually being able to guess—the inner motives of a young woman with so much going for her right here in town?

Gracie loudly cleared her throat, and Kyle was pulled from his musings to discover she was staring at him as if he'd grown two heads.

He shrugged his shoulders and flashed her a crooked, apologetic grin.

"Let's walk to the restaurant," Gracie suggested, stepping one foot off the curb and looking back, eagerly holding her hand out for him to follow and smiling in earnest.

Kyle readily agreed. How could he resist? It was a warm spring afternoon, slightly exceptional for May in Wisconsin, though in fact he wouldn't know personally since this was his first, and probably only, year in the state, having been born and bred in the Lone Star State.

Texas.

Kyle took a deep, ragged breath and forced his dark memories as deeply as they'd go into the back recesses of his mind. Now wasn't the time to be treading back on his melancholy. He'd already been brooding enough in poor Gracie's company.

It was a wonderful, sunshine-filled day, and he was with a beautiful woman. The air was ripe with spring, with the pungent scent of budding flowers and fresh green grass just after its first spring mow.

A man couldn't ask for more blessings than that, now could he?

Gracie, Kyle realized with a start, had been chattering along as they went, while he'd been completely consumed by his thoughts. And, he also realized bluntly, he hadn't a single clue as to what she had said.

She was quiet now, though, observing him with a tantalizing tilt of her head that sent the sunlight shimmering off the highlights of her red hair.

"A penny for your thoughts," she said, her voice rich and warm.

He chuckled awkwardly and jammed his fingers through his thick black hair. "Trust me, Gracie, you don't want to know."

Judging from the jewel-fine gleam in her eyes and the way she cocked her hands on her hips just so, she was obviously going to argue the point, but he quickly cut her short.

"We're at the restaurant," he pointed out, gesturing to the front door of Harry's Kitchen. "And I don't know about you, but I'm hungry enough to eat a whole menu's worth of items. Let's go in and get a table before we end up having to wait."

She pressed her full lips together and surveyed him keenly. "Kyle—" she began, and then stopped without finishing her sentence. She stared at him a moment more, and then said, "Okay. Let's go in."

Relief flooded through him. Thankfully, she wasn't going to press the issue. But that emotion was quickly followed by a surprising surge of another, less familiar feeling.

Disappointment.

"Look, Hart, the whole town must be in here for

lunch today,'' Gracie exclaimed, obviously pleased by that tidbit of information.

Kyle wasn't so sure how he felt. He looked around at the green-upholstered booths of the eating establishment and indeed, there were many familiar faces staring wide-eyed back at him, waving him—and Gracie—inside the door with eager grins.

Feral grins, he thought caustically, at least on some of the older women he knew from church. They'd had their matchmaking eyes on him ever since he'd arrived in Safe Harbor.

In Kyle's mind, and in his newly unattached state, there wasn't a thing in this world more daunting than a group of determined, small-town ladies wanting to hitch a man up to the marriage wagon, and no amount of objection made a difference in their minds, or in their plans. He *had* protested, as politely but loudly as possible, for what little good that did him.

He was a reasonably young, and reasonably—*ahem*—handsome, single man in a small town with an abundance of young, single women. As far as the self-appointed town matchmakers were concerned, he was fair game. No amount of denial on his part would make them see the light.

The only *light* the older members of the Safe Harbor Women's League wanted to see was candles at the end of a sanctuary aisle with a white wedding runner leading right up to it. And him in a tux, smack-dab in the middle of the whole picture.

He could see the news on the front page of the

Safe Harbor Courier already—Wedding Bells Ahead for Dr. Kyle and Nurse Gracie.

It almost sounded like a soap opera. He slid a look at Gracie, but she'd already headed off toward the first table to greet some of her friends. She was grasping hands and hugging necks and kissing cheeks and being her sweet, charming self.

What man wouldn't be proud to walk into a restaurant with a woman like Gracie Adams on his arm?

He smiled in spite of himself. Gracie was animated and pretty, the perfect woman to charm a bitter widower's heart. It was a compliment to him that they considered him dating material for her.

But the Women's League would have to look elsewhere to pair Gracie Adams up.

True, a man would be foolish to not want a woman like Gracie in his life and in his heart.

But Kyle wasn't any man. He didn't have a heart left to give.

She was, he realized, heartache peeling back as fresh as if it were just yesterday and not over a year ago, certainly not anything like his wife Melody, neither in looks nor in personality.

Melody had not even come up to Kyle's shoulder, and had long blond hair and rosy cheeks. She'd been quiet, though not shy, preferring to think things through before she spoke, and then she would speak slowly and calmly, even when things were in chaos.

Though Melody had cheerfully held a job to help see Kyle through medical school, her true passion in life was making a home, baking cookies, sewing gingham curtains and refinishing antique furniture.

The happiest day of her life was the day she'd brought their new daughter home from the hospital. He knew she had dreams of playgrounds and PTA meetings.

But that was not to be. Kyle grit his teeth until he could feel the pulse in his jaw.

A drunk driver had taken all that away from her—from them. Kyle had wanted to give them so much. What else had he been working so hard for?

But his window of opportunity had been taken from him before he'd even had the opportunity to give them a tenth of what they deserved. One man's bad decision had robbed him of a lifetime with his wife and daughter.

So while Kyle had no doubt it was a compliment to him that the older women staring so openly at him considered him dating material for a young woman like Gracie Adams, the Women's League would have to look elsewhere to pair her up.

With a grimace he shifted his gaze—and his attention—back to Gracie, who continued to glide from table to table, catching up with the latest news and gossip from old friends.

Gracie caught Kyle's tolerant gaze for a moment, then turned to the next table, glad Kyle was so easygoing about her taking a few minutes with her friends.

She especially wanted to have a moment to chat with Constance Laughlin before rejoining her handsome lunch partner. She wouldn't say she was avoiding Kyle exactly, but the space to catch her breath was doing her a bit of good.

"Constance. I didn't know you frequented Harry's," Gracie said, leaning down to give the dear middle-aged woman a hug and a kiss on her cheek.

Constance flashed her the same wide-eyed, guilty gaze of a child caught with her hand stuck squarely in the middle of a cookie jar. Dual slashes of pink flushed high on her prominent cheekbones, and she shook her sleek, bob-cut black hair in immediate denial.

Gracie had been half-prepared to be the one to field the question about her handsome *male* lunch companion, the topic at nearly every other table she'd visited.

But Constance hadn't even appeared to notice. At least not yet.

Which could only mean something else was going on. Something bigger.

She lifted her head and scanned the small restaurant, more than a little curious what that *something* could be, but nothing looked out of the ordinary, except perhaps the sparkling eyes of Dr. Kyle Hart. He winked and smiled at her, and her heart missed a beat, then raced like mad to make up for it.

Gracie scowled. The man was far too handsome for his own good. And what was worse, he looked as if he knew something she didn't, something that was amusing him greatly.

For some reason, that annoyed her. And of course, he knew it.

Pursing his lips against his smile, Kyle briefly nodded his head in the direction of the front counter, then slid into the nearest booth.

Again he made the merest nod, then punctuated his gesture with another friendly wink.

Frowning, she turned to see what Hart found so humorous, and spotted Harry Connell, the kitchen's owner, in a muted, heads-down conversation with none other than Nathan Taylor, Safe Harbor's resident mystery man. He had appeared out of nowhere one day, but had been regularly spending weekends in the small town.

Constance's guilty countenance suddenly made perfect, and very romantic, sense. Gracie felt her heart whirl and turn all aflutter as she turned back to her friend, placing her knuckles on the table between them and leaning in with a conspiratorial air.

"Constance Laughlin," Gracie whispered through her teeth, though never losing her smile, "did you have something you wanted to tell me?"

Constance batted her lips and swallowed hard, but the only thing she uttered was a squeak.

"You wouldn't be here with Nathan, now would you, dear?"

Constance's eyes widened and her hands flared up in denial, but after a moment she sighed and leaned back in her seat, clearly resigned to the inevitable.

Gracie laughed, her gaze straying to Kyle for a

moment before looking back at her friend. "You know as well as I do you're practically announcing your engagement to the man just by being seen here with him. You know how the gossip mill in this town works."

Constance's face fell, and Gracie slid in beside her in the booth, putting her arm around her dear friend and giving her a hug, feeling instantly contrite for her words. "You know I'm just joking with you, hon. No one cares if you want to have lunch with Nathan, and it's nobody's business but yours, anyway."

Constance nodded, but there were tears in her eyes. "I know. I just—" Her voice cracked and she fell silent.

"Nobody's rushing you," Gracie assured her, feeling a surge of almost matriarchal tenderness that was at odds with their varying ages. "Besides, I'm definitely playing the trump card on today's lunch hour."

She gestured toward the booth where Dr. Hart was lounging, watching them both with an amused gaze. "Nathan Taylor may be a good-looking man, but why don't you take a gander at *my* lunch date? Talk about setting the tongues wagging..."

"Dr. Kyle?" Constance let out a teenagelike giggle and flickered her fingers at Kyle, whose dark eyebrows shot up into his hairline before he hastily responded with a wave of his own. "Are you telling me that hunk of M.D. is taking you out to lunch?"

She laughed. "I'm taking *him* to lunch."

"Same difference," Constance crooned, her expression only freezing for a second when Nathan slid into the booth across from them. He flashed Constance a special, private smile, her gaze flared for a moment, and a cockeyed sense of normalcy resumed.

"No, it's important that you realize I'm not accepting anything from Hart." Gracie was quick to defend her way of thinking. Speaking helped her feel less like she was intruding on a special moment between two people, which was how she felt when Nathan and Constance looked at each other. "Trust me, there's no fodder for the gossip mill in this room."

Constance flicked her a look that indicated she didn't believe a word of it.

"Kyle and I have a purely *platonic* relationship." She was about to go on and say she'd been the one to invite Kyle to lunch, but then she realized it wasn't true. She might flatter herself that she was the one paying at the end of the meal, but...

He had asked *her*.

A shiver ran through her. She had insisted on paying the tab in order to keep some distance between them. She wasn't sure how she felt about Hart taking the initiative.

Constance, seeing her hesitance, chuckled and gestured to Kyle. "Don't you think you ought to return to your *friend?*" she asked under her breath. "Look at him over there all by his lonely self. You wouldn't want him to get bored and leave without you.''

Gracie flashed a look at Kyle, who looked anything but bored. He was watching her with interest, his eyes sparkling like iced tea in the sunshine and a lazy Texas grin on his face. He casually brushed his jet-black hair off his forehead with his long, supple, surgeon's fingers, and winked as she gaped at him.

Bored, he was not. And he wasn't boring to look at, either.

Her gaze reluctantly returned to Constance, who was smiling as if she were privy to a secret. Gracie mock-scowled and shook her head at her incorrigible and clearly misinformed friend. Clearly there was no reason for Constance to think she was attracted to the man, other than that everyone else was fond of his assets.

''I'll see you Tuesday at the Women's League meeting,'' she said to Constance, and then nodded at Nathan. ''Nice to see you again.''

''You, too, Gracie,'' Nathan replied with a kind smile that lit up his whole face.

Gracie liked Nathan. He was strong but gentle, and she thought he might be sweet on Constance.

It would be nice to see her friend settled down again, Gracie reflected. Constance had lost her husband, Joseph, when rebel forces attacked his camp during a missionary trip to Central America. Since that time she had focused on being a mother, and now a doting grandmother of an adorable grandson.

Gracie, incurable romantic that she was, couldn't help but think maybe it was time for a new romance in her dear friend's life.

Constance had been dating the sheriff, gruff, outspoken Charles Creasy, but Gracie privately thought quiet, enigmatic Nathan was better suited for her friend.

"What were you doing over there, playing matchmaker?" Kyle teased as she slid in the booth across from him and heaved a sigh.

Gracie held up her hands and shook her head vehemently. "I wouldn't presume. I'm sorry to keep you waiting."

"No problem," Kyle replied, taking a long drink of the iced tea he'd served for himself. His eyes twinkled with merriment. "But really, Gracie, do you have to speak with *everyone* in the restaurant?"

Gracie took a sip of her own iced tea, which Kyle had thoughtfully served for her. Harry's was a self-service establishment for the most part, and Kyle had already taken it upon himself to get them drinks, condiments and silverware.

She leaned toward him, her gaze narrowing thoughtfully. She pinched her lips together. "You wanted to create a scandal when you asked me out to lunch today, didn't you?" she reminded him.

He chuckled. "No. I was only kidding when I mentioned the gossip mill, Gracie. But you've certainly sealed the deal for us, either way. I see rings and garters gleaming in at least a dozen eyes. I think we'd better run for the border."

Gracie flicked her hair out of her eyes with the palm of her hand. "I can't help it if people talk. And I can't just ignore my friends and neighbors when I see them in a restaurant or the grocery store."

"Trust me, no neighbor would ever accuse you of neglecting them," Kyle said dryly, trying to smother his grin.

"I'm not going to dignify that remark with a response," she said, tilting her chin in the air as she realized she was doing just that.

Turning her gaze away, she decided to change the subject. Move it off herself and on to something she could handle. "Do you think Nathan and Constance are interested in each other?" she whispered so she could not be overheard.

Kyle glanced at the middle-aged couple. "Looks like," he drawled, sounding amused.

Gracie leaned forward. "I hope so. I know they'd be perfect for each other. She's told me once before that Nathan reminds her of her first husband. Isn't that romantic?"

A flash of pain flickered across Kyle's gaze and Gracie immediately regretted her careless words. But he recovered so quickly, she almost thought she might have imagined his sorrow. His laugh was certainly genuine. "See, you are a matchmaker."

Gracie colored. "Please don't tease me."

Kyle lost his smile. "Gracie," he said, his voice suddenly low. He reached across the table for her hand, giving it a soft squeeze. "You know I only badger you because I like you. I'd certainly never torment an enemy this way.''

He looked as if he were ready to say more, but they were interrupted by one of the waitresses. "Your usual, Dr. Kyle?" she asked after greeting them.

"I'd appreciate that, Maggie," Kyle replied genially, patting his stomach for emphasis.

Gracie guessed she shouldn't be surprised that Kyle frequented Harry's Kitchen, since he was a recently widowed man who probably didn't cook much for himself, but somehow she'd pictured him more as The Bistro type, with fancy cloth napkins and real silver. She knew from talking to him that he'd led a fairly well-to-do lifestyle as a neurologist in Houston.

Maggie turned to get her order. "I'll have the same," Gracie said without hesitation. But the moment the waitress moved away, Gracie asked, "And what would that be, exactly?"

"Would what be?"

"The *usual?*"

"Oh, that." Kyle made a show of licking his bottom lip and patting his flat stomach. "Grilled cheese. Extra pickle."

Gracie made a face.

"You don't like pickles?"

"It's not that. I just expected— I don't know. Caviar or something."

"At Harry's? I don't think so."

Gracie laughed. "You have a point."

"Except…"

"Grilled cheese is such a *boy-next-door* kind of food. You went to medical school."

"And survived on grilled cheese sandwiches. *With extra pickles.*"

"More than survived, I'd say," came a sultry voice from behind Gracie's left shoulder. "Looks to me like you've thrived, big guy."

Kyle clamped his jaw closed, Gracie thought to keep from saying something he'd regret. She couldn't miss the look of pure panic that flashed through his gaze before his eyes glazed over.

Gracie turned to the newcomer, whom she knew well from her schoolgirl years and recognized merely from the sappy sweet sound of her voice. "Chelsea Daniels. What brings you into Harry's?"

"As if you didn't know." Chelsea gave Kyle a long, sliding look that made the man blush.

Gracie rolled her eyes. She'd never gotten along particularly well with Chelsea in school. She had little tolerance for any woman who spent more time combing her shoulder-length brown hair and applying makeup to accentuate her fine bones and delicate features than she did cultivating her friendships.

Chelsea was one of those women who'd matured early, and had always caught the eyes of the boys. And she'd known it. She knew it now.

Always looking after her own self-interests, Chelsea could only be depended on to think of herself and what she wanted.

Now was not an exception; only now, Chelsea

had apparently decided she wanted Kyle. Gracie actually felt sorry for the poor man.

"Are you going on the bachelor's block, Kyle?" Chelsea purred, hovering over Kyle so that he squirmed back in the booth to escape her.

"The what?" he asked, flashing a bewildered and at the same time beseeching look at Gracie. It was clear he had no idea what was going on.

"Oh, never mind," Chelsea snapped, typically and easily annoyed and diverted. "It's really too bad I'm already finished eating, or I'd join you," she said, blowing out a huff of breath. "But there's always another day, right?"

"Uh…right. I guess," Kyle agreed, looking to Gracie as if he were wishing he didn't have to say anything at all.

"Until then…" Gracie suggested, raising her eyebrows and nodding her head toward Chelsea's neglected table of friends.

Chelsea didn't take her eyes off Kyle for a moment. She preened and puffed and purred. "I'm looking forward to it."

"Don't tell me, I don't want to know," Gracie said immediately as Kyle slid upright in his seat again. For emphasis, she put her elbows on the table and placed her palms over her ears.

"It's not my fault," Kyle denied heatedly, reaching across to grab Gracie's hands away from her ears, pulling them to the tabletop and cradling them in his own. "I have no idea what I ever said to that woman, but for some reason, she has it out for me, big time.''

"I wish you two all the best."

"Please don't say that," he groaned, twisting in his seat as if he were in physical pain. "Gracie, you've got to help me get out of this."

"Look, if Chelsea Daniels has her claws out for you, she's going to get you. At least that's been my experience in the past."

Kyle pursed his lips tightly, and Gracie wasn't sure whether he was scowling or trying to bite back a laugh. "And how is that, exactly?"

"You know the type. Popped the boys' eyeballs out of their heads in junior high and never looked back."

"Early bloomer, huh? Do I detect a note of jealousy here?"

Gracie snorted. "Not in this lifetime. I have never, nor do I ever desire to be, the self-indulged type of woman Chelsea has grown into."

"Don't worry about it," Kyle muttered, half under his breath.

"Though in her defense," Gracie continued, not knowing how to take Kyle's comment, "she does get every man she sets out to win."

"Well, that's not how it's going to happen this time."

Gracie cocked an eyebrow, her heart hammering in her chest.

He shrugged. "I only want to be left alone. I'm not in the market for a relationship. I've seen Chelsea around town, and bumped into her at various functions I've attended with the McGuires. She's made it pretty obvious she's interested in me.''

''I'll bet.''

Kyle nodded once, briskly. ''I've tried to tell Chelsea how I feel, but she won't listen to a word I tell her.''

Gracie bit back a token of disappointment. She didn't know what she'd expected him to say, but that wasn't exactly it. ''I'm not surprised, Kyle. She doesn't give up on an idea easily.''

''Speaking of ideas, what was that about a bachelor's block or some such?''

Gracie chuckled and took a long drink of iced tea. ''Wouldn't you like to know? You'll find out soon enough, big guy. You'll find out soon enough.''

Chapter Two

Gracie arrived at the Safe Harbor Women's League meeting Tuesday afternoon to a completely unexpected round of applause. She dropped into a graceful curtsy and then cocked her hands on her hips and looked around, carefully eyeing the handful of women, most of whom she'd known all her life.

"Thank you very much," she said wryly, tapping her foot methodically against the floor. "Now tell me what the applause is for."

"As if you didn't know," Wendy McGuire said with a laugh, smoothing a hand across her burgeoning pregnancy. "Talk is all around town about you and that hunky Dr. Kyle."

"Me and Dr. Kyle what?" Gracie rasped, though she wasn't entirely surprised by her friends' reaction. There wasn't enough going on in Safe Harbor to keep everyone really busy, so they grabbed at whatever they could for amusement. She was as guilty as anyone in this room about reaching for what seemed exciting news wherever she could find it. "Sorry to disappoint everyone, but Hart and I are just friends."

There was an audible groan at the news, and Gracie chuckled loudly. "Do you gals want to try that one again in unison?" she teased.

"Does this mean you won't be bidding on Kyle's chocolate at the bachelor's block auction next Saturday?" teased the newly wedded and extremely happy Annie Simmons-Mitchard.

"Assuming, that is, that I can get him up on the block at all," Constance complained good-naturedly as she passed out miniature plastic pacifiers in pink and blue, each tied with a ribbon long enough to dangle around a woman's neck like a necklace.

"Is he being stubborn?" one of the women called, hooting in displeasure.

Constance shrugged. "Kyle hasn't said yes, yet, but don't worry, ladies. I've made sure there are enough men up for auction this year. Everyone here will get their box of chocolate."

There was a pleasant round of laughter and a few raucous comments. "Well, Gracie, is it chocolate for you or not this year?" Wendy prompted, returning to the subject Gracie had hoped was long forgotten. "Assuming Kyle takes the plunge."

"I believe I can safely promise *not* to bid on Hart's box of goodies," Gracie assured everyone, holding up her right hand, palm open. "The playing field's wide-open where that man's concerned."

"Never say never, sweetheart," came the crackly old voice of the town's postmistress and biggest gossip, Elizabeth Neal.

Gracie spotted her a catty grin, and the old woman cackled pleasantly. Elizabeth Neal, and Safe Harbor residents in general, would learn soon enough that she and Hart had nothing more in common than a working relationship.

No box of chocolates was going to tempt *her,* even if they were held by strapping biceps and accompanied by the tempestuous amber eyes and the alluring knockout smile of Dr. Kyle Hart.

"Isn't this party supposed to be for Wendy?" she loudly reminded those present. After adding her gift to a large pile, she chose a spot beside Constance and took her seat with a sigh.

The lighthouse meeting room was appropriately decorated with pink and blue streamers, and a long table had been ornamented with a cow jumping over a bright sliver of a moon. Wendy was having her third baby, but the Women's League insisted on throwing a baby shower for her, even so.

"Do you know if it's a girl, Wendy?" It was Elizabeth who asked aloud the pointed question everyone was wondering in their heads. Robert and Wendy were the proud parents of two boisterous boys, ages six and four; soft, sweet and pink were all the keynotes on the Safe Harbor question list where the McGuires were concerned.

Wendy rested a hand on top of her abdomen and chuckled happily. "Robert and I have decided to keep it a secret until the birth."

She held up her hands at the murmurs of protest that rose at her words. "I know, I know. You'd think by number three, we'd want to know, and the sooner, the better. But you know, there are too few real surprises in life, at least good ones."

Gracie thought Wendy's explanation sounded reasonable, and actually a bit romantic at the core. But she could tell by the groaning and variety of expressions around her that everyone in the room didn't share her opinion on the matter.

"Do you have a feeling one way or the other, on whether it is a boy or girl?" Gracie asked, then unconsciously brushed her fingers over her own trim waist. "Not that I would have the slightest notion if such a thing were possible."

"Well, I haven't been dangling rings over my belly, if that's what you mean." There was general laughter over Wendy's referral to the old wives' tale of rocking and circling rings. "However, if I were to guess, I'd guess I'm carrying a *boy*."

Constance groaned loudly, and Gracie elbowed the middle-aged woman playfully in the ribs.

"Well, how would you like to have all boys?" Constance whispered. "I only had one, and he was all I could keep up with."

Unexplainably, a crystal-clear image of three adorable black-haired, amber-eyed ragtag boys wrestling with each other entered her head, and she smiled softly. "That might not be so bad."

"I wouldn't mind another boy," Wendy said, and Gracie wondered if she'd heard Constance's comments. "My little guys are the light of my life. Besides, it's just a feeling. Robert thinks it's a girl. The baby is a gift from God, whether a boy or a girl," she reminded them softly.

"Of course," Gracie agreed, darting a glance at Constance. "What matters is that the baby, boy or girl, is born healthy."

"From your mouth to God's ears," agreed Wendy, squeezing her eyes closed for a moment.

The party quickly got under way, and the women played a couple of goofy baby shower games that Gracie would just as soon have skipped, but seemed to be perennial favorites of the old-timers.

They guessed the length of yarn needed to wrap around the mom-to-be's waist. They matched famous mothers and children from history—Gracie won that one, and received a pretty crystal candle holder in the shape of a swan.

And then there was the one Gracie disliked the most—anyone caught saying the word *baby* lost the pacifier around her neck to the lucky woman who'd heard the word uttered. Gracie was far too much of a talker not to say the word *baby* at a baby shower, and it annoyed her to have to try. But she was a good sport, and since she could only lose her coveted pacifier necklace once, it didn't stop her from talking up a storm.

Robert was supposed to be in charge of picking up the cake from the local bakery, but he had not yet arrived with it, so the ladies settled in to some good, old-fashioned gift opening.

"You handled that whole Dr. Kyle thing pretty cleanly," Constance said, leaning in for a conspiratorial whisper.

"Hart? How's that?"

"You know what I mean." Constance nudged her playfully on the shoulder.

Gracie chuckled. "Yes, I guess I do. I'm glad they believed me, that Kyle and I are just friends."

"Oh, no, sweetie, they don't believe you. *I* don't believe you. We're just being polite and giving you rope to hang yourself."

Gracie narrowed her eyes on her friend. Why did no one believe her? "Thank you very much for your encouragement."

Constance giggled and pecked her on the cheek affectionately. "Don't worry, hon. You'll figure it out soon enough."

Gracie nodded. "Let me know when, okay?" she commented wryly.

Constance smiled, but it slipped. Gracie saw her friend's expression falter, reached for Constance's hand and gave it a squeeze. "Enough talking about me. How are you doing?"

"I guess I shouldn't be panning advice. It's not like I'm an expert." She curled her hands in her lap, then glanced away, pretending to take interest in the gift Wendy was opening.

"You're obviously better at this than I am," Gracie pointed out, trying to lighten the mood. "No one said a single word about you and Nathan today. What's your secret?"

Constance pinched her lips. "No one would dare. Seriously, I think people walk on eggshells when they're around me. *I* walk on eggshells around me. I don't know what to do."

"Because?" Gracie prompted.

"Because—" Constance paused, her gaze darting around the room as if looking for an avenue of escape. Finally, she looked back to Gracie, her eyes bursting with panic, like a cornered animal. "I'm attracted to Nathan. From the soul."

Constance's confession made the air freeze in Gracie's lungs. There was something in what she said that went beyond the mere romantic, a connectedness there that was almost spiritual in nature.

Gracie could *feel* it. For once in her life, she was speechless.

"Nathan reminds me so much of my Joseph," Constance explained softly, her voice coarse with emotion. "That's terrible to admit, I know, but it's true. I don't know if that's why I'm attracted to him. I do know that's why I *shouldn't* be."

The silence was deafening. Gracie could hear Wendy wadding up a piece of wrapping paper, and the sound was magnified in her ears until it was like roaring, until she wanted to cringe.

To have a love like Constance had had with Joseph, and for God to take that away, would be the most terrible thing she could imagine happening to a person. And now, to be tempted with a man who looked and acted like the man you had lost?

How could a woman handle that magnitude of pain? How could she stand to be alone?

"I'm waiting," Constance said, the gleam back in her sapphire-blue eyes. "You're supposed to be giving me advice."

Gracie felt her jaw drop, and she found herself doing something she hadn't done much of late—praying. Praying to God for guidance, for words of wisdom to give this dear friend. Because Gracie's own words, her own realm of experience would be nowhere near enough. She didn't have the words to say.

She closed her eyes and took a deep breath, focusing. "I know what my eyes see," Gracie said at last.

"And that is…"

"You like Nathan. The relationship you have with Chief Creasy is— Well, I'll let you and Chief Creasy work that out. But don't deny your heart, Constance."

She took a breath and laid a comforting hand on her friend's arm. "My head is all awhirl today with talk of bachelors and babies and one's true love. But I do know this. God is in charge of it all. And even though it seems really confusing to you and me, He's got it all going around the way He wants. And in the end, it all boils down to what's in your heart."

Tears glistened in Constance's eyes, which shone

like jewels against the pale skin of her cheeks.
Gracie felt a new rush of emotion for her friend, and
threw her arms around her in a big hug.

"Gracie, dear heart," Constance said, hugging
her back, "those are wise words for one so young.
I do believe I'll take you up on them. I've been
sitting on the sidelines for too long."

Gracie hardly thought she'd been sitting on any
sidelines. Constance had not been the type of
woman to tuck herself away and grieve for what
she'd lost. She'd put her loss to good use, to helping
others. She'd started foundations and charities, and
even this Women's League itself.

But Gracie supposed there was love.

"I'm terrified," Constance continued, "but I
know when I need to look a challenge in the eye.
And I will. It's you I'm wondering about."

"Me?"

"I want you to promise me one thing, young lady,
before you leave here today."

"What's that?" she asked, feeling at the moment
like she could promise the world. It was the least
she could do after seeing the bravery of her own
friend.

"Promise me you'll take your own advice. When
the time comes for *you* to love, and it soon will be,
don't be afraid to follow your heart."

"You're scaring me."

Constance merely grinned.

"Anyone for cake?" Gracie was surprised by the
deep, familiar baritone. It wasn't Robert McGuire

brandishing the bakery cake. What in the world was Kyle Hart doing at a women's meeting?

His gaze met hers as she stood and whirled away from where he was. Panic set in as her instinct told her to put as much distance between herself and the good doctor as possible. But Constance was trailing her, and she knew there wasn't much chance of that.

"Robert needed to see a patient at the clinic and asked me to deliver it for him," she heard him explain to the crowd. "I hope I'm not too late for the party. I couldn't get away until now."

"You're right on time, Kyle," Wendy assured him. "And you must stay and join us for a piece of cake."

Constance grabbed Gracie by the arm and pulled her toward Kyle. Gracie dug her heels in, but it was no use fighting against her determined friend.

"Dr. Kyle! You're looking particularly handsome this afternoon," Constance crooned. "What a lovely suit you're wearing." She greeted him with a friendly kiss on the cheek.

Kyle chuckled, but it was clear to Gracie that he was uncomfortable with Constance's blatant perusal and adamant praise. He cleared his throat, then pulled at his collar and conspicuously loosened his tie. "Uh, thank you. I think."

He cleared his throat. Again.

The man was shy!

Gracie's eyebrows shot through her bangs. Who would have known?

Here he razzed her to death without the least care

in the world, and yet when he was teased, he hemmed and hawed around with Constance like a regular retiring Southern gentleman.

Gracie couldn't hold back her smile. Especially when Constance grabbed at the tie Kyle was loosening and made him turn all red in the face.

At least Kyle didn't have Chelsea to contend with. She wasn't much for spiritual things and didn't think boring meetings with what she considered a bunch of old ladies were worth her time.

"The thing is, Dr. Kyle…" Constance pulled at the end of the silk tie, making it snug once again against Kyle's neck. Gracie could see the muscles in his skin vibrate as he swallowed hard. "The thing is…this weekend is Memorial Day Weekend."

Kyle nodded.

"You'll be here."

Kyle nodded again.

"And we'll be here." Constance leaned in for the kill. "And guess what? You're going to have the wonderful privilege of helping out the underprivileged this weekend."

"Don't you just love her way with words?" Gracie quipped, holding back a laugh.

Kyle, of course, looked totally confounded, as well he should. Constance was leading him like a bull by the nose, and with good reason. The poor man didn't stand a chance against her.

But even Constance couldn't just go up to a man like Kyle and ask him to—

Well, it sounded pretty ludicrous, even to Gracie,

and she'd been participating in the bachelor's block since she'd been old enough to hold a box of chocolates in her hand or make a winning bid.

"It involves chocolate," Constance was saying. "And charity."

Kyle nodded politely. "I'm happy to help, ma'am," he said with his cute little Texas drawl. "Just tell me what needs doing, and I'm on it."

Gracie choked on a sip of punch. "Actually, hon, you *are* it."

His gaze fixed sharply with her own. "I beg your pardon?"

"What Constance is trying in her roundabout way to say is that Uncle Sam wants you for the Memorial Day bachelor's block auction, Monday morning at ten o'clock sharp at the gazebo in the park."

"The what? For whom?" he sputtered. His jaw dropped, and he looked from woman to woman as if they'd both lost their minds.

Fortunately, she and Constance were both enjoying the moment far too much to take his looks seriously. His adorable confusion and muddled expression was worth a thousand words.

"Not Uncle Sam, precisely," Constance clarified with a chuckle. "We're making money for the Safe Harbor Family Practice Mercy Fund. For the poor in Safe Harbor who are without medical insurance. These are people, primarily women and children, who would go without medical aid were it not for this fund."

"I know what the Mercy Fund is for," he said

dryly. "I work with these people on a daily basis. Robert and Gracie introduced me."

"Good," Constance said with a relieved smile. "Then I'm sure you won't mind helping out."

"What I *mind* is auctioning myself off like a piece of—*meat,*" he said with a groan, shoving his fingers through his hair. He winked at Gracie. "I'm just not that kind of man."

"Oh, don't worry, it's nothing like that," Constance assured him. "Nothing sordid you'll be ashamed to be a part of."

"Is that so?" he drawled, sounding not at all convinced.

"Remember, Doctor, Safe Harbor is a small town. We're dignified and fun-loving. All you have to do is to show up and bring a box of chocolates. We'll auction you and the sweets off to the highest bidder, and you'll spend the rest of the day escorting a nice young lady about town. Now how hard could that be?"

Kyle shot a look at Gracie that clearly conveyed what he really thought—the bachelor's block sounded like sheer agony. But he shrugged and said, "Okay, I guess. For charity."

"For charity," Constance agreed merrily, planting another kiss on the young doctor's cheek. "Don't worry, you won't be sorry."

Constance immediately skipped off to speak to a nearby group of women, no doubt to plant another seed for charity. Gracie took another sip of her punch and watched Kyle over the top of her cup.

"I already am sorry," Kyle murmured, taking a sip of his own drink.

"What was that?"

"Nothing," he muttered.

"Don't worry, you'll live."

"Does she do that to everyone?" he asked, gesturing toward Constance. "I've never felt so bull-dogged in all my life."

"Constance?" Gracie shrugged and nodded. "Pretty much. She's really amazing. She's a wonder with organizing things. She's almost single-handedly turned this town around since she arrived over five years ago. She's gotten us all involved in any number of charity projects."

"Like bachelor auctions," he said with a groan, sounding none too happy.

"Well, if it makes you feel any better, every other year, it's a bachelorette auction."

His eyes lit up with interest. "Yeah? Does that mean next year I get to bid on you?"

Gracie's eyes met his, which were filled with warmth and humor, and something else she couldn't quite put a name to.

Silently, she asked him the question she was afraid to voice aloud.

Next year?

Chapter Three

Memorial Day dawned brand-spanking bright and fresh as the birth of a newborn babe, full of sunshine and the pungent scent of spring flowers, everything a man could ask for in a holiday morning.

And it dawned far too early, in the opinion of Dr. Kyle Hart.

If he had his way, it would be snowing today.

Wisconsin was known for its late-spring snow-storms, wasn't it?

Why couldn't such a happy phenomenon as snow in springtime happen today?

But no.

It had to be the perfect day for a picnic.

Kyle winced as he tightened the knot on his bow tie and surveyed himself critically in the half mirror over the sink in his bathroom.

He'd said he'd be at the bachelor's block auction

today, and he would be there. But it wasn't going to be an easy day. And he knew he wasn't going to like it, no matter what Constance or Gracie or anyone else said about it.

Constance Laughlin had indicated he could wear whatever made him comfortable, from jeans to a sport coat; but in the end, he'd opted for his classic black tux, deciding he would give whatever lady bid on his chocolate the first-class afternoon she deserved. And he guessed he wanted to be different than the run-of-the-mill Safe Harbor man standing on the block.

Now that he had his tux on, though, he wasn't so sure he'd made the right choice. For one thing, this was Safe Harbor, Wisconsin, not Houston, Texas. And he was going to a Memorial Day picnic, not a black-tie affair at a five-star hotel. He wanted to be different, but he didn't want to show anybody up.

Besides, the suit reminded him a little too much of his old life, before he moved to Safe Harbor, when dressing up used to be the norm. When the pursuit of the almighty dollar had come at a devastating cost.

He'd lost his wife and his sweet, little infant daughter.

He glanced at his watch.

Whether he liked it or not, he was due at the bachelor's block at the park.

Or more precisely, *on* the block.

He chuckled as he made his way to his full-size, extended-cab white pickup truck, a throwback to his

Texas days. He was making way too much out of what was surely a really small subject.

How bad could it be?

The green on the hill was already filled to overflowing with the residents of Safe Harbor when Kyle arrived at the park. Some folks milled around setting up picnic tables and stoking up grills, while others stood in groups talking with old friends, or threw Frisbees or footballs to each other.

It was a tranquil scene, something eminently small town. It was the sort of thing a painter would capture on canvas.

Kyle knew he'd never see such a gathering in Houston if he looked for a year. There was always an air of commerce in the big city, even when no one was selling anything.

Here, everyone looked genuinely relaxed. The air was fairly buzzing with anticipation of what the day would bring.

This was what he'd come to Safe Harbor for, this sense of belonging to something bigger than himself, and Kyle eagerly joined in, greeting those people he knew from the clinic. And he was more than happy to gulp down an early hot dog with Robert, Wendy and their two active boys, though it was only nine in the morning.

Constance checked in with him, reminding him of his ten o'clock obligation—as if he could forget. And Chelsea fluttered by to remind him—or was it to threaten him—that she intended to make the highest bid for him and take him home with her.

He could only hope some other Safe Harbor lady would take pity on him.

And while the news that Chelsea was after him like a fly to honey flustered him, it was even more troubling that he continued to scan the crowd without spotting so much as a glimpse of the flame-colored hair he was desperately watching for.

Where was Gracie?

Somehow, he thought he'd be able to get through this whole auction thing better if she was around for moral support.

And he'd just assumed she'd be here today, so much so that he hadn't even thought to ask her outright. She was far too much of a social butterfly to miss such a big community event, and her heart and soul were in Safe Harbor.

She'd *be* here. She had to be.

He thought to ask Robert if he knew where Gracie was, but decided against it. He didn't want to call attention to the fact he'd noticed Gracie's absence, much less that it bothered him.

Kyle knew there were already rumors circulating, speculating on the relationship between Gracie and him. He didn't want to stoke it up.

Besides, he knew Robert would use it as an opportunity to razz his old buddy, as he had done through all their years in medical school. All he needed was the extra ammunition, and Kyle wasn't about to provide the fodder outright.

A barbershop quartet started singing a familiar gospel tune at the gazebo, which was Kyle's cue to line up for the bachelor's block. He straightened his suddenly tight bow tie and cleared his throat.

Ready or not, he was about to make his modeling debut, and it was a paid engagement.

He joined the group of his uncommon associates, most of whom he knew at least by sight, if not by name, behind the gazebo. Not a one of them looked half as nervous as he felt.

Constance was fretting about, consulting the clipboard in her hand and lining the men up elbow to elbow, then changing the order with a shake of her head; adjusting a shirt collar here, straightening a lock of hair there, mumbling under her breath all the while.

"Nervous?" he asked the man standing next to him, a young carpenter named Buck something-or-other who had done some work at the clinic.

"Hmm? Naw. Been doing this for years. Or at least, every other year." Buck laughed at his own joke.

"No big deal, huh?"

Buck shrugged. "Guess it all depends on who bids on your chocolate."

Kyle chuckled dryly, then coughed as it stuck in his throat. "I was afraid of that."

Buck pounded him on the back and roared with laughter. "If you could see your face, man. I'm just kidding around with you."

Kyle wasn't so sure about that, but he didn't say so. There wasn't time. Constance was checking everyone's chocolate. Some of the men had brought big, frilly heart boxes full of chocolates or truffles, and Kyle wondered if he'd made a mistake in his choice of a single chocolate rose.

Kyle was third in line, and listened with interest as the crowd, which sounded mostly feminine, got warmed up. What started as mild cheering and clapping soon became whooping and hollering, and it sounded like the men on the block were egging it on.

So much for small-town and dignified. He was going to end up looking like a fool in front of all those women. He couldn't do this.

He wished for the millionth time that Gracie was here with him. At least she'd have something silly to say that would make him smile, make him forget about this ironic mix of comedy and tragedy.

He heard his name announced and stepped forward before he lost his nerve. He guessed he wasn't completely surprised to find they'd built an actual *block* in front of the gazebo, to showcase the men and their chocolates. Three stairs led up to the platform, and Kyle reluctantly climbed to the top.

The view would have been intimidating to a total extrovert, which he wasn't. While there were a fair share of men in the crowd, he was certain every single woman in the town was present for the auction.

Every woman except one. The only face he really wanted to see in the crowd.

Gracie Adams.

He was going to have to do this without her he

realized yet again, and his disappointment that she still wasn't here to support him was surprisingly sharp and bitter.

He scanned the crowd, wordless and unmoving. He didn't know whether he was supposed to make a speech or flex his muscles, so instead he just lifted his hand and wiggled his fingers in an awkward, simple wave to the crowd.

The women on the green immediately exploded with applause.

He cracked a grin.

"I bid fifty dollars," came a high-pitched, squeaky voice from the front row. "Move over, ladies, because that man is mine."

Kyle barely restrained himself from cringing and hopping right off the block. Actually, he wanted to run for his life.

The voice belonged to Chelsea. He nonchalantly grit his teeth and coached himself to remain on the block. For the sake of charity, he was going to be a gentleman, no matter what kind of sacrifice he was called on to make.

People oohed and aahed at the high starting bid, but there was even more surprise when an elderly woman in the back promptly followed with an animated, "Seventy-five dollars."

Chelsea's face turned a hearty shade of pink. She crossed her arms, shifted from foot to foot, and looked genuinely miserable for a good moment before she called out, "One hundred dollars!"

She sounded none too happy about having to

name such a high figure. It was obvious she'd intended to win his chocolate and his time on the strength of her opening bid alone.

With the purplish look on Chelsea's face, Kyle thought he might be close to causing a riot, just by his being on the block.

He grinned in earnest. This might be fun.

After the first minute or two of being gawked at and fussed over by a large crowd of women, he began to lose the self-consciousness that had first held him back.

As the bidding continued to rise in twenty-five dollar increments, he found himself playing to the crowd. He was having fun. The women were clearly enjoying themselves. And the bids were going up, up, up.

From the look on Constance's face, Kyle was pretty sure bids usually didn't top three hundred dollars, and they were almost up to five. As crazy as Kyle thought the whole idea was, the Mercy Fund was really going to benefit, and a lot of poor people would be able to get medical attention.

It was only a moment later when Kyle sensed a sudden shift in the atmosphere, a marked tension crackling through the air that changed everything.

The bidding had wound down to three determined women—a couple of feisty senior citizens Kyle thought must be bidding away their social security checks and Chelsea Daniels. His determination to be a gentleman weakened as Chelsea acted less and less like a lady.

His preening and primping turned to hemming and hawing. He reached for the end of his tie, giving it a firm yank. Anything to relieve the sudden pressure he was feeling around his neck.

He realized too late that his gesture had the unintended effect of egging his admirers on. He'd not considered what loosening his tie would suggest to the innocent—or not so innocent—onlookers, both those bidding and those simply cheering him on.

Heat rushed to his face. He was making a muddle of this. Things were going downhill so fast it was almost a landslide.

Could it possibly get any worse?

Gracie shifted, carefully adjusting her perch on a thick branch in a sturdy oak tree at the edge of the green, straining forward to get a better vantage point of what was going on.

Specifically, she wanted to see Kyle squirm on the bachelor's block.

She was late getting to the picnic because she'd been helping out an indigent family on the dock who'd called her when they'd had a minor medical emergency. She couldn't—and wouldn't—turn this family down, but she hoped she had not missed the spectacle she was sure would occur when the good doctor made his debut.

She'd relied on an old childhood trick, one she had learned when she was six years old and which had stood her in good stead over the years—shimmying up a convenient tree to get a better lay of the land.

Her mother had called it tomboyish and unlady-like. She'd always thought it rather practical, herself. And now was certainly no exception. She wasn't going to be able to get a glimpse of the gazebo any other way.

After nimbly shifting down to her stomach on the tree branch, her knees braced around the rough bark for security, she was finally able to get a good glimpse of Dr. Hart.

Gracie watched Kyle shrug back into his jacket and attempt without success to retie his bow tie. She got the unspoken message, even if the other women cheering on the green didn't hear what he was silently trying to tell them with his actions.

He didn't want to be paraded around like a piece of meat. And though he was going along with it like the gentleman he was, it was killing him to do it. From the tortured look on his face, he'd like to be anywhere but here in Safe Harbor, and most especially not on the bachelor's block.

Suddenly, Gracie found herself experiencing feelings she never thought to encounter when she climbed up this tree on the green.

She felt sorry for Dr. Hart.

She'd always been outrageously outgoing by nature, and she'd grown up in Safe Harbor, after all, with their strange traditions and irascible characters. It was all she'd ever known, and she was perfectly comfortable in this uncommon little part of the world. Up to and including taking her stand on the bachelorette block when it was her turn to do so, even flirting with the fellows to get a good price.

But Kyle was different. He came from another world entirely. He was educated, distinguished, refined. He wasn't some hick right off the farm who looked at the bachelor's block as his opportunity to make his mark in the world.

Her heart swelled into her throat. She could almost physically *feel* Kyle cringe from where she crouched in the tree as Chelsea made yet another bid. Gracie knew how much it cost Kyle not to jump right off that block and make a run for it.

The next moment, her decision was made, and her heart was firm.

She swung her leg around and shifted down, swinging herself so she was dangling on the branch from her arms, where everyone on the green could see her, if—when—they looked in her direction. There could be no mistaking what she was about to do.

"One thousand dollars," she said, her voice as crystal clear as her mind was made up, and as her heart was strong and true.

"The doctor has been sold. To me."

Chapter Four

Kyle had never been so relieved in his life. "I could kiss you," he told Gracie as she approached to redeem her prize.

He handed her the chocolate rose with a bow and a flourish, laughing when she colored and snatched the rose from his grasp. "I'm *going* to kiss you."

With that, he quickly leaned over and planted a noisy kiss on her cheek, knowing it would take only a moment for her to become indignant.

Or rather, more indignant. She already looked like she was agitated, from the beautiful pink color in her cheeks and the way her eyes were shining. It made Kyle want to smile.

"Hold that pose," said a voice at their side. Nathan appeared suddenly at their side, and flipped open a large sketchbook. He quickly began sketching the pair of them with a stick of charcoal.

"I didn't know you were an artist, Nathan," Gracie commented, obligingly offering her cheek up to Kyle so Nathan could finish his picture. Whatever else Gracie was, she was a community woman, and she put her own desires aside to placate the good of the whole.

It was one of the things Kyle liked best about her, one of the traits he most admired.

And he wasn't about to look *this* gift horse in the mouth. With amusement brimming over in his heart and, he was certain, in his expression, he pulled out one side of his black tuxedo jacket as if to slyly hide the both of them, then pressed his lips once again to Gracie's soft cheek, this time pausing long enough for Nathan to get what he needed on paper.

"You two make a fine couple, you know," Nathan commented cheerfully, tipping his sketchbook so Kyle and Gracie could see the completed drawing.

"Just beautiful," Gracie said softly, brushing her fingers just shy of the paper, tracing the lines of Kyle's jaw.

"You sure are," Kyle agreed, feeling extra generous with his praise as he saw how well Nathan had captured Gracie's classic features in charcoal. "Look at that smile."

"Like I said," Nathan agreed with a knowing grin and a nod, "you two are great together."

Nathan started to stride off, sketchbook in hand, no doubt eager to capture other moments of Safe

Harbor Memorial Day fun, when Kyle jogged to catch hold of his sleeve.

"Listen, man," he murmured lowly, so Gracie couldn't hear what he was saying. "What are you going to do with that picture?"

Nathan's eyebrows shot into his hairline. "This? Why, I don't rightly know. Did you want it?"

"Can you frame it for me?" Kyle asked, knowing he was asking the older man to go the extra mile. But somehow, here in Safe Harbor, it didn't seem too out of place to make such a request. "I can pay you. I'd like to give it as a gift."

"To Gracie." It wasn't a question and was accompanied by Nathan's wide, friendly grin. There wasn't a hint of condescension, only kindness.

Kyle smiled back. "Of course."

"Then it's on me. Would you rather I deliver it straight to Gracie, or would you like to do the honors yourself?"

"I appreciate that, Nathan. I'll be glad to pick it up from you. Just name the date and time."

"We can meet next Sunday after church. How's that sound?"

"Thanks again," Kyle said, jamming his hands into his pockets as Gracie approached.

Nathan excused himself rather abruptly and again made to leave.

"What's going on?" Gracie queried brightly. She was clearly suspicious.

Kyle shrugged. "Nothing."

"Nathan is quite a guy, huh?" She was still tapping him, but with more subtlety.

"He is," Kyle agreed. That part, at least, was the solid truth.

Now it was time to change the subject. "And so are you. Where can I take you today in order to show you my heartfelt appreciation? The Bistro and a movie? Or would you rather go dancing?"

Gracie laughed and shook her head. "Don't get your hopes up, big guy. I only bought you because I felt sorry for you."

Kyle knew his face was growing as red as the blister on his ego, and struggled to contain both. He'd known at the outset that Gracie wasn't just any woman bidding on the man in the tux like the rest of the women had been—but *ouch!*

She'd really stabbed him where it hurt. He responded in kind before he thought better of it.

"Let me write you a check." He overcompensated his gestures as he reached inside his coat for his wallet. "I'll pay you back for every dime you bid on me. Then I can just thank you politely for your help, and be on my merry way."

This time, it was Gracie coloring. "Don't you dare, mister. I knew exactly what I was doing when I made that bid, and now I'm following through on it. Without your help."

He shrugged, half sorry he'd stepped on her figurative toes, half enjoying the interchange. "This isn't your typical bachelor auction, is it? Aren't you the one who pointed that out?"

He paused and jammed his fingers through his hair. "I don't know what you want, Gracie. You're going to have to tell me, in plain language, in words of two syllables or less, because I can't even begin to guess. And frankly, I don't really want to try."

Gracie cocked her hands on her hips. "What do I want?" she repeated, sounding a little angry, and just a little bit coy.

Kyle sighed loudly and waved his hand in the air. He wasn't positive he should be happy to see the gleam in her eyes.

"I want you to change your clothes."

"I beg your pardon?"

"Your clothes. For what I have in mind, a tuxedo won't do at all."

Kyle straightened his bow tie, which Gracie had retied for him only moments before. He was supposed to be her escort for the day. "What? But I thought…"

"Well, we're not going on a date, Kyle, so you can relax."

It took a moment for her words to sink in, for him to think through all the implications. And then, oddly enough, he did feel like relaxing.

A little, in any case. "Okay. I'll change. Then what?"

"How much gardening did you do back in Texas, by the way?"

That question caught him off guard. "Absolutely none. I hired someone to keep the grounds for us," he reminisced with a tentative grin.

Her auburn brows dropped low over her eyes. "I was afraid you might say that. I'm not much of a green thumb, myself."

Suddenly she shrugged and the smile returned to her lips. "Oh, well, I guess we'll have to wing it. We're two bright people. We'll figure it out, I'm sure. I've got some books we can look at. I need the manpower, and you need to work off your time."

"Do my *time?* You make this sound like a prison sentence."

"Hard time," she teased, her eyes glowing. "Are you wishing Chelsea had won you? I'm guessing you'd be tucked away at some romantic candlelight meal for two by now."

His gaze snapped to hers, and his shock evidently must have shown blatantly on his face, because she roared with laughter.

"No?"

"No," he assured her hastily. "Trust me, gardening suits me just fine."

Tailoring his words to his actions, he scribbled down directions to her house and took off for his own apartment, where he quickly changed into a pair of old blue jeans and a loose black-and-gray T-shirt. As an afterthought, he slicked a comb through his hair and slapped on some aftershave.

Then he caught his reflection in the mirror over the sink and laughed. What was he doing? He was just going to get dirty and sweaty, digging in the dirt.

Gracie would make good and sure of that. A thousand bucks worth of sweat.

He grunted and shook his head at his own reflection, then jammed a pair of sunglasses into the neckline of his T-shirt, pushed the crown of his black felt cowboy hat onto his head and shrugged into his genuine black leather jacket.

This was twice today he'd spent more time than absolutely necessary thinking about his own appearance. He'd have to watch himself or he would be going on downright vain.

He was still laughing at himself when he arrived at Gracie's house. He was surprised to find she lived in the older and more stylish segment of Safe Harbor, Harbor Hills. The sprawling estates were built in brick and fenced in white, and looked wide and open and welcoming to Kyle after the cramped confines of the fancy Houston condo he'd lived in as a young, single surgeon. There he'd been able to hear his next-door neighbors argue well into the night.

Even when he and Melody had purchased a house in the old, rich hobnobby part of the city, the generous architecture had been built close together— feet separating each dwelling instead of the free-roaming acres he experienced as he drove the winding country roads here in Safe Harbor.

People not only owned dogs and cats here, but a few had goats, donkeys, horses, and he even saw one house with llamas on his drive up the winding hill. It was a different world.

Gracie was waiting for him on the front porch steps of the sprawling redbrick ranch-style home, one arm wrapped around her jean-clad knees and cradling a tall glass of lemonade in the other. Her red hair swirled around her bare shoulders in the breeze, above the lime-colored tank top that set off her coloring perfectly.

She was, in Kyle's mind, the absolute picture of country sweetness and elegance.

She took his breath away.

Kyle swallowed and settled his gaze on the lemonade. He found he was suddenly parched.

Gracie apparently hadn't missed his perusal. Grinning, she gave him a blatant once-over with gleaming eyes, then saluted him with her glass. "The leather jacket is a nice touch. And the lemonade is right over there on the table."

Kyle found a cold jug of lemonade and a tall, chilled glass right where she pointed, on a small round table at the shaded end of the porch. He poured himself a glass and drank it down all at once, then filled his glass once again.

"I haven't even put you to work yet," she teased, standing to move beside him. "Being at auction must have been harder than I imagined."

Kyle groaned. "You have no idea."

"Trust me, you'll earn it."

Gracie immediately produced a shovel and showed him to the backyard, where she'd staked off a large area in order to plant a garden.

The dirt all had to be turned, Gracie explained.

This was her first attempt at a garden, but she was determined. She'd borrowed books from the admittedly limited Safe Harbor library, and studied them carefully.

"Don't they have machines for these kinds of things?" he asked Gracie as he began the daunting task, spading and turning what seemed like infinitely small shovelfuls of earth when compared to the gigantic rectangle Gracie had staked out.

Gracie shrugged. "I'm sure they do. A rototiller, I think it's called. But isn't it so much more fun to do it this way?"

Kyle stopped digging and leaned an elbow on the shovel, cocking an eyebrow when she shrugged again and clamped her mouth shut.

"Well, isn't it?" she asked again, her eyes widening hugely.

He narrowed his eyes on her. Something was not quite right, here. "Gracie, what kind of car do you drive, again?"

"A Focus. Why?"

"I've got a truck. Let's go." He dropped the shovel and reached for her hand, pulling her toward the front of the house.

She pulled back and set her heels in. "Wait! Where are we going? My garden isn't finished!" she protested, but it was weak, and they both knew it.

"We're going to town. Specifically, to the hardware store to rent a rototiller. My treat. I'm even going to haul it for you."

Surprisingly, Gracie didn't argue. She even let

him help her into his truck, boosting her up with his hands spanning easily around her small waist.

"You have a beautiful home," he commented as they made the short ride into town. And I like the area. "Have you lived there long?"

Gracie gave him a long, probing look before she answered. "All my life." She paused again before adding, "It's my parents' house, actually."

"Oh? Your parents are away serving as missionaries somewhere in South America, right? I don't think I've met them."

"Quito. Ecuador."

Kyle didn't think he imagined the hint of irritation in her tone, and decided to dig a little deeper. "What exactly do they do there? Translate the Bible into Quechua or something?"

Gracie sighed loudly, as if it pained her merely to talk about it. "Dad writes for an international radio station and my mom DJs for them. They reach people for Christ all over the world by shortwave radio."

Kyle's eyes widened in surprise. Now, at least, he could guess at why she sounded resentful. He knew full well her own deepest dream was to leave Safe Harbor to become a missionary herself. "So why aren't you with them?"

Gracie propped her chin on her palm and stared out the side window. "I was still in high school, and they wouldn't let me go. They said it was too dangerous. They said I wouldn't have the opportunities in Quito that I have in Safe Harbor. They said I had a life of my own to pursue.''

''You do,'' Kyle reminded her softly. He suddenly felt like a very old man, seeing Gracie here with her whole future spread out before her, completely untouched and full of potential.

He wanted to say the words again, as if that would make them any truer. When he glanced into her eyes, he saw an awkward, insecure girl who didn't realize her school days were long behind her.

But that wasn't Gracie.

Was it?

Maybe she had other reasons.

''Why haven't you joined them?'' he asked softly, shifting his gaze to her from time to time.

Her wide-eyed gaze pummeled him, and he immediately looked away from her. Not fast enough to miss the way her jaw dropped in astonishment, however.

''Are you crazy? I can't just leave.''

He wanted to ask her why she thought she couldn't leave to join her parents, but he wasn't *that* crazy. He kept his mouth closed and his eyes on the road. For some reason, she didn't see that she only had to step out and do whatever was in her heart to do. She was still young enough to sweep up the world if she wanted it.

Unlike his own life, which had already been maxed out at age thirty-seven. He'd already experienced a lifetime of grief. He just wanted to live what was left of his life in quiet obscurity.

He didn't want to risk loving again because he didn't want to risk losing again. And while he knew rationally that one didn't inevitably follow the other, it wasn't a risk he was willing to take with his own heart.

Gracie was a different story.

But he didn't pursue the subject with Gracie, at least for the moment. For one thing, she didn't look like she was in the mood for advice. And for another, loading the rototiller into his truck wasn't as easy as it looked, and quickly took up his attention.

But Kyle tucked the information away in his mind, determined that in the right place, at the right time, he would find out why the beautiful, vivacious Gracie Adams refused to embrace what could be an exhilarating and high-speed future.

Gracie shifted from her seat on the sofa and tried once again without success to peek into the kitchen to see what Kyle was up to. He'd seated her on the sofa well over an hour ago, and while he'd come in occasionally to offer her a drink or a moment of conversation, he was hush-hush about what was going on in the next room.

Gracie couldn't identify the aromas teasing her nostrils now, and that only intensified her need to know.

After the rototilling was done, Kyle had loaded the bulky machine back in his truck, downed another glass of ice-cold lemonade and made ready to leave. Gracie had been surprised, and a little offended, that he seemed in such a hurry to leave. They'd shared such a nice afternoon together—or at least she'd been of that opinion, until she saw Kyle's odd behavior.

And then, at the last moment, with one foot already in the cab of his truck, he leaned his elbow on the clean white top and grinned at her with all the charm he possessed. And no matter how she tried, she couldn't help it—her heart was immediately ready to forgive the man anything.

He'd knocked twice on the roof of his truck and told her not to make plans—that he would be back in about an hour.

She didn't know what to think.

And she really didn't know what to think when he showed up just over an hour later laden down with paper bags from the grocery store, a variety of colorful fresh fruit peeping from the tops of the bags.

She'd asked him what he was up to, but he'd simply herded her into the living room and made her put her feet up, which was where she now sat. He'd turned on the television for her, but she hadn't been able to keep her interest in any of the shows.

She was too interested in what Kyle was doing in the kitchen. She'd deduced, of course, that he was attempting to fix her dinner. She thought it was cute.

Suddenly, Kyle was standing before her, a towel draped across one arm. His hair was wet and slicked back, and his face had the rose-colored, fresh-scrubbed look of having been just washed up.

He reached for her hand and helped her to her feet. "Your dinner is served, madam."

"Thank you, Jeeves," she teased. "My, aren't I being spoiled today?"

"You haven't seen anything yet," he promised her, the moment before he swung her around the corner into the dining room.

Gracie gasped in surprise and pleasure. Kyle had really outdone himself.

Her mother's large, formal dining room table was covered with a white lace tablecloth, and antique brass candlestick holders held taper candles that set the room off with a pleasant glow. Kyle had set the table with her mother's china and silverware.

"I found the china in the hutch," Kyle said, obviously having followed her gaze. "I hope your mother won't mind. I promise I'll wash it by hand when I'm finished up with it, and I won't break anything."

Gracie laughed. "Trust me, Mom wouldn't mind. She always uses the china on special occasions. In fact, I think she'd be impressed. I have to say that I certainly am. What is all this food?"

A variety of aromatic dishes lined the table, only some of which Gracie could identify. All of them looked as if they had been prepared with a gourmet touch, and all of them looked delicious.

"You sound like you were expecting boiled hot dogs," he said dryly, though any offense in his voice was clearly put on for her benefit.

Gracie bit back a smile. "Or bagged salad. I'm

sorry. I have to admit I stereotyped you. Successful big-city doctors don't usually have to cook.''

"I don't have to cook. I *like* to cook. It's my hobby, and I've been pursuing it for over ten years. Hard to believe, I know, but I'm a gourmet chef in my spare time."

-"Phenomenal."

"Well, you know what they say...."

"What do they say?"

He chuckled and held out her chair for her. "The proof is in the pudding, my dear. You can decide how you feel about my *hobby* after you try my cuisine."

Gracie seated herself and allowed Kyle to push her chair in, then waited until he'd seated himself at the opposite end of the table.

"What is all this?" she asked, picking up the first dish, chicken and rice that she thought might smell of curry, and spooning a sample onto her plate. "I'm sure there must be some explanation to such an exotic variety of dishes."

His eyes gleamed. He leaned forward, waving the taco he'd clearly forgotten he was holding in one hand. "Oh, there is an explanation, Gracie. That's the best part of the meal."

"Better than candlelight and good company? I highly doubt that."

"Look around you. You've got dishes from all around the world. I fixed Thai food, something from the Philippines, Italian, Sudanese and even Australian. Oh—and of course I couldn't forget the Mexican food," he said, lofting his taco in a salute.

"Australian food?" she said, picking up on his last statement. "I don't think I've ever heard of Australian food."

He chuckled. "Well, don't worry. It's not alligator or snake meat."

She spooned a helping of an unidentifiable casserole onto her plate, wondering if this was the Australian dish in question.

"Only emu."

The serving spoon hit Gracie's dish with a clatter. "Emu?" she shrieked.

He roared with laughter. "Kidding. Kidding. But the look on your face, Gracie!"

She made a face at him. "Go ahead. Laugh at my expense."

"You're going to have to open your mind to new things when you leave Safe Harbor to become a worldwide missionary," he said, scooping food with one hand and forking it into his mouth with the other. "I'm sure your parents have brought you some interesting dishes from Quito. But who knows when you'll be called on to eat lamb eyeballs or worms or something."

"*Must* we talk about this while we're eating?" Gracie asked, looking down at her plate that once looked appetizing and now only reminded her of lamb eyeballs and worms.

"No. We can talk about whatever you like. I just

thought you'd enjoy a taste of the world, as a small sample of what's coming to you in your future.''

She sampled the Australian casserole. She still couldn't identify the meat or the spices, but she wasn't sure she wanted to. It literally melted in her mouth, and it was delicious.

''I hope my future is half as good as your cooking,'' she said around another bite of food. ''Because I don't think I've ever tasted anything as good as the meal I'm eating right now.''

He looked genuinely delighted. Gracie was surprised that her opinion meant so much to him, but she couldn't help but smile back at him when he grinned at her across the table.

They ate quietly for a while, softly conversing about nothing and everything. Kyle introduced his dessert, a chocolate mousse he said was a complement to the auction she had won. A little extra chocolate on the side for the sweetest lady he knew.

Gracie didn't really believe all Kyle's sweet talk, but she enjoyed it. He was easy to be around, even when he was teasing her, which was most of the time. And he really listened when she spoke.

There was a connection between them, something emotional. And spiritual. Gracie could feel it, and she wondered if Kyle could feel it, too.

''I looked for you this morning,'' Kyle said, spooning the soft chocolate and smooth whipping cream into his mouth. ''I was hoping for a friend in the crowd. But I didn't see you at all—at least until you suddenly flipped out of that tree and made a bid for me. Where were you, anyway?''

Gracie studied her dessert for a moment. ''I was down at the dock.''

''The dock? What's wrong, Gracie? You didn't know that the party was in the park? How long have you lived here already?''

Gracie chuckled. ''Believe me, I knew where the party was going on. And you know how much I like to schmooze with the neighbors.''

Kyle pushed his dessert cup aside and leaned on his arms. ''Whatever you were doing, it must have been important.''

''It's not a state secret,'' Gracie said softly, twirling her spoon in her chocolate. ''It's just that no one has ever been interested enough to ask me what I was doing before.''

''I'm interested.''

She could see by the expression on his face that he was serious. She smiled softly and launched in. ''When I go down to the dock, I'm actually visiting the dock district, the poorest area in Safe Harbor.''

''People live down there?''

''Mostly single women with children. There are so many children down there.''

He lifted an eyebrow. ''And you were down there this morning because…?''

''Because I was helping out an indigent family with a minor medical emergency.''

Kyle ran a hand across his jaw, looking thoughtful. ''I'm not surprised,'' he said slowly. ''But I am impressed by what you are doing. You should be commended for helping these people."

Gracie held up her hands and shook her head vehemently. "Oh, no, don't start heaping accolades on me. I do this because it needs to be done. Because it is the least I can do to help."

His golden-eyed gaze locked with hers. "I understand."

Somehow, she thought that he did. Again, she felt a sense of connection with him.

"Does this have anything to do with the Mercy Fund?" he asked, leaning forward in interest.

"No. I do this on my own." She paused and curled a lock of hair around her finger. "These are the folks who would benefit most by using the Fund, but many are too proud to use it."

"Even for their children?" he asked, his voice low. He was obviously struggling to keep amazement from his voice. Not judgment, Gracie didn't think.

"They aren't bad people."

"I never said they were."

"They don't want what they consider a government handout."

"But they'll take help from you?"

Gracie nodded.

"I want you to take me there, Gracie." His words were so low she barely heard what he said.

"Really?" She was a little bit surprised, and very pleased by Kyle's announcement. "You would go with me sometime?"

"I would go with you next Saturday, if you'll let me. Or at least on the soonest convenient Saturday. You just tell me what to bring, and I'll be on it."

Gracie chuckled. "I'm really excited to be able to share this part of my life with someone. I think you'll really be blessed by it, Kyle."

"I'm blessed any time I'm with you," he said, his voice constrained.

"Will you cut it out with the compliments, already? I think I've had my thousand dollars' worth. You can relax now, and forget about the auction."

"My compliments were real. And they had nothing to do with my supposed obligation to you. However, that does bring up an issue."

"What issue?" Her stomach began swirling with butterflies at the way he was looking at her, as if he had more secrets to share, and that she ought to be prepared for anything.

"The money. Please tell me it's not next month's rent."

She laughed and shook her head. "No. Nothing like that. I take a little money out of each paycheck and put it in savings."

"For?"

She shrugged. "Travel. Whatever I come up short on with my missionary support."

He had an odd, thoughtful look on his face, and she was afraid he was going to ask once again to pay her back. She was determined not to field such a question.

But instead, he asked her, "Did you enjoy your dinner?" he asked. "And your dessert?"

"You know I did."

What was he getting at? He was smiling with his eyes, but his mouth was a firm, straight line.

"Well, I imagine most of the ladies who bid on the gentlemen on the block got dinner and a movie, at the very least."

She shrugged. "Something like that. But I've already told you that you don't have to feel obligated to fulfill any obligations where the auction is concerned. I gave the money to charity. And to rescue you from Chelsea Daniels," she added with a laugh.

"And I am eternally grateful," he said. "I simply want to express that gratitude. You have to give me that, anyway."

Suddenly, Kyle pushed the chair backward and stood to his feet. He walked toward her without a word, and stood by her for several seconds just looking at her, almost in suspended animation.

A smile flickered on his lips as he held out his hand to her. "Dance with me?"

Gracie chuckled and shook her head, her heart fluttering rapidly in her throat. "There's no music, Kyle."

"Ha!" His eyes glittered with amusement. "I knew I forgot something when I was setting everything up this evening. Music to set the mood. Why didn't you say something before?"

"I didn't notice."

And she hadn't. She'd been too wrapped up in spending time with Kyle.

"Well," he said, smiling in that toothy, charming way he had, "if I rectify that little oversight, will you dance with me?"

The look on his face was surprisingly vulnerable, as if he were afraid she might really turn him down. Gracie couldn't speak, she was so surprised by that token of emotion, and how much it said about the man underneath the veneer.

He didn't wait for her to answer, but swung around and strode toward the stereo in the living room, a huge, multispeakered system that was her father's pride and joy. Kyle fingered though her parents' CD collection and groaned. "Lawrence Welk?"

"Big band is the ultimate in dancing music," Gracie reminded him with a laugh, in a bright, singsong voice that was not her own. "At least that's what my parents keep telling me."

Kyle groaned again. "Not for this cowboy."

Gracie could have put him out of his misery immediately and brought out her own eclectic collection of CDs, which included some of the latest country bands, but she was far too much enjoying poking fun at him and seeing him squirm.

She tapped her chin with her index finger and pretended to think. "You know, they might have some Barry Manilow...."

"Wonder what's on the radio?" he suggested

swiftly, changing the switch to FM and jiggling the dial against the static.

"Hmm. Yes, what?" She smiled softly at his hurried antics.

With another twist of the dial, a slow country ballad crooned from the speakers, and Kyle grinned at her in triumph.

"A little late, but still somewhat effective, don't you think?" He walked back to the table and held out his hand to her again.

As she stood looking up at the handsome man, his warm golden eyes glimmering in the candlelight, the sudden sense of where she was, in the house she'd grown up in, about to step into the waiting arms of a very attractive, mature man, sent her fight-or-flight instinct into full battle array.

A silly, juvenile, *frightened* part of her wanted to dash down the hallway and lock herself in her room, away from the warm glow of Kyle's eyes and from the strength of his arms. She'd never encountered such strong feelings for a man before.

It wasn't that she hadn't dated—she'd gone to homecoming and prom, and though she had kept her mind on her work during nursing school, she had dated a couple of local men over the years since.

Just not seriously. And in her mind, they could hardly be called men. She had grown up with them, gone to school with them. Kyle had lived most of his life in a big city, and had seen and experienced things she'd only dreamed of.

Not to mention the fact that he'd had a wife and

child. She wasn't sure she knew how she should act, or even react. She wished for a moment her mother or father was here to get advice from.

But they weren't here to help her, and in truth, she didn't want them to be. Because as her heart settled down out of her throat and her brain stopped blaring its incessant warnings into her ear, she realized that this was Dr. Kyle Hart, her trusted co-worker and a good friend.

She wasn't a confused teenager anymore. She was a full-grown adult, and the feelings she was experiencing were genuine.

She stepped into his arms without a word.

He pulled one arm snug around her waist, and tucked her hand in next to his chest with the other, where she could feel the rapid beat of his heart. He was an excellent dancer, with a natural, graceful rhythm that was easy for her to follow.

After a while, he began to hum along with the song, and then to sing softly in a rich baritone that left Gracie's knees weak. She closed her eyes and laid her head on his shoulder, for the moment perfectly content breathing in the leathery scent of his aftershave and hearing the soft rumble of his voice in her ear. She didn't know the words, but she didn't have to.

She knew he was singing her a love song. And she wished it could last forever.

But it didn't, as she knew it wouldn't.

The beat ended, and there was a long moment of dead air space. Kyle stopped dancing, and Gracie froze, suddenly feeling awkward within his embrace. She didn't know what to do with her arms, which were wrapped around his neck, her fingers in his thick, luxuriously soft hair.

Kyle didn't seem in a hurry to let her go, even as a twangy country two-step came on. His arm was still strong around her waist, his breath warm on her shoulder as they stood unmoving together.

His other hand slowly moved up her arm and across her shoulder to caress her cheek, to gently tip up her chin so he could look into her eyes.

''Gracie,'' he said, his voice coarse and husky. His breath was coming in short rasps and his eyes were warm with emotion. ''I haven't held a woman in my arms since my wife passed away. I...''

Her throat closed and she thought her lungs might burst from lack of air.

She knew what he was asking. It was in his gaze, if not his words.

After a moment, she nodded.

His jaw worked, and he swallowed hard. Then he nodded, too, and smiled as he gently framed her face with his hands.

In the blink of an eye he closed the distance between them, and when he kissed her there was nothing tentative about his actions. Kyle Hart was a passionate man. It showed in his work at the hospital, and it showed now in his touch.

Gracie melted into his arms, her whole heart singing with joy.

For a split second.

And then she froze solid as a deeply familiar lilting Irish brogue pressed through the haze of her mind, shattering the moment.

"I'll thank you to be getting your hands off my only daughter!"

Chapter Five

Instinctively, Kyle tucked Gracie behind him, putting himself between her and...*whoever*. He knew by the way she had stiffened that he needed to protect her. Even though everything was still sort of hazy in his mind, he struggled to make sense of what was happening.

He'd been kissing Gracie, lost in the sweetness of her lips, when...

Slowly, the man's words penetrated the fog in Kyle's mind.

Get your hands off my daughter.

His *daughter!*

Kyle blinked and stared at the glaring intruder. The portly, white-bearded man with gleaming green eyes *could* be related to Gracie, even if he reminded Kyle more of Santa Claus.

Though Kyle didn't think Santa Claus would be

looking quite so serious about things, with a frown that bordered epic proportions underneath his beard.

Gracie snagged an arm around Kyle's waist and peered out from underneath his arm, making his emotions toward her swirl in his chest.

"Daddy," she said, clearly surprised. "What are you doing here?"

The man placed beefy fists on his hips and narrowed his gaze on his daughter. "I think the question, young lady, is what are *you* doing?" He paused dramatically and shook his head. "Here?"

Gracie stiffened even more in his embrace. Kyle tightened his arm around her, instinctively rallying behind her, if not exactly taking her side in the matter. He could hardly do that, yet.

He didn't even know what the sides were. Only that the lines had been drawn.

"You must be Gracie's father," Kyle said, thinking to intercede on what was obviously a volatile situation. He'd always considered himself good at diffusing difficult moments, and this one was a doozy. "I'm Dr. Kyle Hart, a friend of Gracie's."

The man's bushy white eyebrows hit the ceiling. "Is that all you have to say for yourself? That you're a friend of Gracie's?"

Kyle's own brow furrowed as he struggled to respond. "As opposed to what, sir?" he asked finally, knowing the question sounded belligerent, but at the moment, not particularly caring.

"Douglass Joseph Adams, stop harassing the good doctor this instant." An attractive, petite, middle-aged brunette stepped into the room and pushed her husband aside with the flick of one hand.

She turned to Kyle with a smile and a warm hand of greeting. "Dr. Hart, we are very glad to meet you. Please don't pay the least attention to my husband's grumbling. He still thinks Gracie is six years old and is dancing on his toes."

She chuckled as if she were visualizing the very word picture she had created, then continued. "He hasn't figured out yet she's a grown-up woman on her own, with her *own choices* to make." She gave a pointed look at her husband, and then slid her gaze over to Kyle. "I'm Madelyne, by the way."

"Thank you, Mother, for coming to my defense," Gracie said wryly, arms akimbo. "Now can we please stop talking about me and get to the important stuff, like what in the world is going on here? What are you doing home so soon? I thought your official furlough wasn't for another month yet, in July. Or am I the only one here who is all confused?"

That, at least, explained Gracie's obsession with planting the garden and getting everything at the house looking good. One mystery solved, but only a small victory, Kyle conceded mentally. Gracie was a riddle within an enigma, and he wasn't even close to figuring her out.

Which, he had to admit, only made her that much more appealing.

Kyle looked from mother to daughter, noting the striking similarities between them. Gracie may have gotten her Irish coloring, that flaming red hair and her sparkling green eyes, and even her height from her father, but the straight, classic nose and strong cheekbones clearly came from her mother's side of the family.

And maybe her striking good looks. Mrs. Adams was clearly every bit as beautiful as her daughter, and still held her own sparkle.

"Brad and Carrie Hackman have decided to leave our missionary team at the end of the year," Gracie's father said gravely, his bass voice coarse. He coupled his hands behind his back and began pacing, which made Kyle very nervous.

Gracie made a high, squeaky, surprised sound and grasped at Kyle's arm, as if for support. Kyle felt a primitive, male, protective urge well up inside him, and he stepped an inch closer to her and draped his arm around her shoulders.

"Permanently?" she asked softly, stepping into the safety of his shoulder. She looked composed on the outside, but Kyle could feel her shaking where his fingers brushed her waist.

Douglass frowned and nodded, then stopped pacing and faced them. "I'm afraid so. Carrie just discovered she has developed multiple sclerosis. She must return to the States to care for her illness."

Kyle felt Gracie stiffen for just a moment before she rushed to take her mother's hands. "I can't believe it. What an awful thing to happen. This must be so difficult for you."

Gracie put her arm around her mother's shoulders but addressed Kyle. "The Hackmans have been working with my parents since they first joined the missionary team in Quito. They are my parents' mentors, and taught them everything they know about being on the mission field. And then, over the years, they have become some of our dearest family friends.''

"They have, indeed," her father agreed with a solemn nod. "And they have been dealt quite a blow with this latest news, though they are taking it one day at a time, with faith. We would do well to keep them in our prayers, most especially Carrie, of course."

"But why are you home early?" Gracie asked. "The Hackmans aren't leaving Quito until December."

"As you can imagine, things have been quite chaotic," her mother said, patting Gracie on the arm.

"Yes," Douglass agreed. "We obviously should have given you some warning we were returning," he said with a pointed look at Kyle. "But it wouldn't be too much of an exaggeration to say we hopped on the first plane back here. We thought it would be a nice surprise for you."

Kyle, who had drifted to Gracie's side, nudged her when she didn't respond to her father's obvious implications.

"It is," Gracie said belatedly. "A surprise."

"The missionary society we work for has a new young couple they've been grooming. Originally, the young people planned to work in the Ukraine, but now they're taking a crash course in Spanish and are going to join us in Ecuador. We're here to help them train.''

''And the Hackmans?'' Gracie asked.

''Have remained in Quito,'' said her father. ''The less Carrie has to travel, the better.''

''Do they have children?'' Kyle asked, thinking about how little ones would be affected by their mother's extended illness. He wondered if a woman in such a position would be able to keep up with the strenuous demands of motherhood.

''Two,'' Madelyne said with a gentle smile. ''A boy and a girl.''

Kyle frowned.

Madelyne shook her head, as if reading his mind. ''They're both in college. Not that it won't be hard on them, too, of course, but they're old enough to offer help to Carrie now that she needs it. They won't add to the burden.''

''Both fine, Christian young people,'' Douglass commented, half under his breath.

Kyle saw Gracie go stiff again. She had just started to relax, and Kyle wanted to sigh in exasperation. Or maybe give a good cowboy holler.

''Say what you mean, Daddy, and get it over with,'' Gracie said, her voice tight and high with held-back emotion.

Her father grunted and shook his head. ''I'm not saying anything, missy, and you won't be getting sassy with me, even if you are a grown lady, as your mom seems to think you are.''

Gracie took a deep, ragged breath, but didn't reply. Kyle couldn't tell whether that was because she was carefully masking her emotions, or whether she simply couldn't think of a clever reply.

Though the latter certainly wasn't like the Gracie he knew.

Douglass planted his beefy fists on his hips and leaned forward. "But I am still wondering," he said in that booming, yet lilting bass voice of his, "what exactly it is I came upon when I walked into my very own house this evening."

Kyle immediately stepped forward, intent on being the one to explain the innocence of the evening's activities, and to put to rest any misconceptions that might be lingering as to what was going on, but Gracie nudged him in the ribs with her elbow.

Hard.

"Not that it's any of your business, Daddy," she said, her voice challenging, "but Kyle and I were having dinner together."

"Dinner for two, I'd say," Douglass commented gruffly, waving his hand toward the dining room, then tugging on his beard.

"Does anybody feel like coffee?" Madelyne burst in with an overly cheerful voice. "I certainly could use a stout cup of java myself right about now."

"I'll help." Gracie reached for her mother's hand, and together they quickly and efficiently promenaded from the living room.

Gracie didn't even look back.

Kyle guessed he couldn't really blame her for

making a quick exit, even if she didn't bother to take him with her. He supposed he would have taken any out he could get under the same set of circumstances.

Her father sure wasn't one to let up on a situation. Or a person.

And now, Kyle realized with a start, the man's low-browed, pinch-mouthed attention was firmly and completely focused on *him.*

Douglass sat down on an easy chair with a huff of breath, then motioned impatiently for Kyle to take a seat on the couch. Which he did, though he sat stiffly on the edge of the cushion, as straight-backed and rigid as a military man.

"So, what's the weather like in Quito?" Kyle asked, rubbing his knees with his palms and trying—he thought perhaps without a great deal of success—for a light tone to even things out a little bit. He was surprised at just how nervous he was, and reschooled his emotions to deal with Gracie's father man-to-man.

Douglass took a long, uncomfortable moment to consider before he answered. When he did, it was low and brusque. "Temperate."

Which was not, Kyle thought, how one could describe Gracie's father's frame of mind. No wonder Gracie couldn't break herself out of Safe Harbor.

This whole situation with Gracie, her struggle with herself and her situation, was all beginning to make sense to him. She wasn't a twenty-seven-year-old woman hanging on to her mama's skirt strings;

she was being smothered to death by an overprotective dad.

"I think I've heard a little bit about Ecuador," he said, continuing the outward dialogue, however sparse on Douglass's part, while he continued to sort things out in his mind. "Doesn't it stay in the sixties and seventies year-round?"

"Temperate," Douglass repeated, not taking his eyes off Kyle for an instant. Suddenly, he leaned forward and plunged a hand through his thick white mane of hair, which Kyle knew once must have been the rich red color of Gracie's.

"I want to know what your intentions are toward my daughter," he said without further preamble. "And I want to know now."

The man had been skirting the issue since the moment he'd burst in the door, but his forward, old-fashioned way of putting things still took Kyle off guard for a moment.

He'd known he'd stepped from urban madness into small-town peculiarity when he'd come to Safe Harbor, but now he was stepping right back into the twentieth century and into a situation for which he was completely unprepared—never mind for which he had an answer to.

"Mr. Adams, sir—"

"Douglass," Gracie's father corrected gruffly, still not taking his eyes off Kyle, who wasn't even sure the man blinked. "I think, under the circumstances, we ought to be on a first-name basis, *Kyle.*"

Kyle stiffened. He didn't like the way the man used his name at all.

He was half expecting Douglass to pull out the proverbial shotgun and demand a wedding on the spot for the man who had been caught errantly kissing his daughter. It was just that kind of surreal situation.

"What are your intentions toward my daughter?" Douglass demanded once again, tugging sharply on the tuft of his beard.

Kyle opened his mouth to speak, but not a single word came out.

The truth was, he didn't *know* what his intentions were toward Gracie. He hadn't thought that far ahead when he kissed her. It was one of those impulsive things that had just happened.

One thing he did know, whatever else might or might not be: he cared for Gracie.

He hadn't touched a woman since the tragic death of his wife and baby daughter in a car accident. He couldn't even think of it.

Until now.

Until he was dancing with Gracie, and remembering their intimate conversation over dinner, and how her eyes lit up when she talked of her ministry among the dock people. How rich and warm her voice was, especially when she was angry or excited. And how her perfume, an exotic orchid blend, smelled when his face brushed against her hair.

And how he couldn't *not* kiss her when she tipped her face to his.

What was there to tell?

He looked blankly at Douglass and closed his mouth, shrugging mildly to indicate he had nothing to say. Nothing Gracie's father would want to hear, or Kyle would want to admit.

"I'll have an answer on this." It sounded mildly like a threat, except that for some reason Kyle couldn't get it out of his head that Gracie's father really *did* look a lot like Santa Claus, and who could feel threatened by Santa Claus?

"Douglass, leave the boy alone." Madelyne Adams, smiling and bustling around in a frilly apron, reentered the room bearing a tray laden with steaming mugs of pungent coffee.

A grin tugged at the corner of Kyle's mouth despite his discomfort. It had been a while since anyone had referred to him as a *boy*.

Madelyne served him a mug of coffee and a knockout grin. She winked conspiratorially, and the hair rose on the back of Kyle's neck. Why did he have the feeling he was being left out of the loop on something? As if she thought she was sharing some kind of secret with him, something Gracie's father did not know?

"I'm not trying to be unreasonable," Douglass insisted, sipping noisily at his coffee. "Nothing unreasonable about trying to seek answers to some commonsense questions, here."

"Of course you aren't being unreasonable, dear," Madelyne agreed, giving Kyle a doting smile. "I would never suggest such a thing. But there's no need to rake the poor doctor over the coals when he's already declared himself.''

Kyle was on the verge of asking her what he'd supposedly *declared* when the full meaning of the overly archaic words hit him like a freight train running right into his chest.

He might as well have been sucker punched. He couldn't breathe, couldn't speak and he wasn't absolutely certain his knees weren't knocking. He tried to buck up, but couldn't seem to find the focus.

''Well, then, I guess that makes everything all right. I guess it does. Everything all right,'' Douglass repeated. He tugged on his thick white beard and looked from his wife to Kyle, a thoughtful expression on his weathered face. ''And a fine welcome to the family we've given you, now, haven't we?''

That did it. Kyle stood abruptly, sloshing hot coffee onto his jeans. He danced about, trying to keep the steaming liquid from his skin, while at the same time maintaining a semblance of dignity. ''I'm not sure where you got the impression that I—''

Gracie rushed into the room like a whirlwind, flying around her father and literally into Kyle's arms, making him forget all about hot coffee. ''I need to talk to you for a minute. *Now. Alone.*''

She was herding him toward the front door as she spoke, and she was obviously brooking no arguments. Kyle put up a token protest to being pushed around, but he let her bully him out.

For as much as he wanted to put Gracie's parents

straight on a few matters, even more did he desire to have a few words with Gracie.

Alone.

So he allowed her to pull him from the room, and followed her out and around the house, back to the newly tilled garden area they'd planted earlier that day. The smell of fresh soil laced the air. The sun had set, but Kyle could still see the muted tones of Gracie's glossy red hair in the twilight.

She looked beautiful. And as nervous as a mother cat with a new litter of kittens.

"Do you want to tell me what this is all about?" he asked when she didn't speak right away. He couldn't wait to hear the answers she would give to the incredible situation she'd put him in.

Even Gracie wasn't that creative.

She frowned and put her hands on her hips. "You sound just like my father."

"You know I'm not trying to do that, Gracie," he said softly, patiently reaching out to brush a strand of her silky hair away from her cheek and twirling it lightly around his finger. "But I think you owe me an explanation for what's been going on here. I'm still guessing on some points, but I'd say I'm pretty involved, at least enough to require a full explanation. Don't you think you owe me that much?"

She sighed loudly and ran a hand down his arm. "Oh, I suppose I do. I never meant for any of this to happen. I just hope you won't hate me when you hear what I have to say."

Kyle chuckled, and his heart welled with emotion. The woman didn't know even half of her appeal. "I think I can safely say I won't hate you, Gracie. I could never hate you."

Gracie nodded fervently, and then swiped a hand across her chin. "Good. I'm glad to hear it. Then it won't bother you that I told my mother we are…" She paused for a moment and looked around, her expression a little wide-eyed and frantic, as if gauging whether or not she could make a dash for it if what she said turned out wrong.

Then she looked back at him, her eyes gleaming with a singular determination. "…*engaged*," she finished bluntly.

"If we are *what?*" Kyle choked out, unable to believe his own ears. It was all adding up now—the way her mother had been acting in the living room with the coffee. How her father had backed off so quickly and had suddenly become so neighborly.

But what didn't add up was Gracie.

"Now why would you tell your mother something like that?" Part of him wanted to shake some sense into her, except that she already looked so completely miserable. Obviously, she was regretting whatever game she was playing.

"I don't *know* how it happened. Honestly. Mom was pushing me to tell her about you, about how we met and how long we'd known each other."

She glanced up at Kyle, then looked away again. "Not like Dad pushes. She wasn't implying we were doing anything…."

She stopped as color flooded to her cheeks. "...we weren't doing anything wrong."

"We *weren't* doing anything wrong," Kyle said mildly, stuffing his hands in his pockets to keep from wringing her neck, or his own.

"No, of course not. But I'm sure you can see how backward my dad is about everything. And my mother—well, she just wants to see her only daughter settled down and married. She wants grandchildren."

Kyle nodded solemnly, and rocked back and forth on his toes as he tried not to crack a grin. "Practically an old maid," he agreed dryly.

She swiped at his arm and laughed.

It was good to see her laugh. She was taking all of this far too seriously. Though Kyle hardly knew what to make of it himself, he knew they could work it out, if they worked together.

Gracie reluctantly continued. "I just looked into my mom's eyes, saw how desperately she wanted me to be settled, and for once in my life I wanted to do the right thing. And I thought about how much I've disappointed her in the past, and how many times I've done the wrong things...and I—lied."

She paused and swept both hands through her hair. "I didn't know what else to do, so I lied. There. I said it. Go ahead and read me the riot act. I'm ready to hear how awful I've been."

Kyle cocked his head to one side, studying her face intently, trying to read what was really going on in that mind of hers.

Somehow, he didn't think it had much to do with having babies in order to satisfy her parents' errant desire for grandchildren.

Much more, he suspected, was in the idea that she'd somehow let them down. That she hadn't done the right thing.

"So what are we going to do now?" he asked softly, folding his arms over his chest and narrowing his eyes closely upon her, hoping to find clues to the real state of her mind.

"We?" she asked, her voice no more than a high-pitched squeak. Her gaze flew to his and her green eyes locked with his. "Do you mean that?"

His eyebrows hit his hairline and he coughed twice to dislodge the sudden lump that had formed in his throat. Once again he felt as if he'd been thrown somewhere off the continent. "Do I mean *what?*"

"That you'll pretend to be engaged to me." She blurted the words out so fast Kyle hardly knew if he heard her correctly. But the spritely look on her face told him that he had. Especially when she added, "Only for a little while."

He bit on his bottom lip for a moment, considering exactly what he wanted to say. What he wanted to do. It was a touchy situation, one he would never have considered possible, and frankly, his own emotions were all over the map.

On one hand, he could feel Gracie's desperation, even if he couldn't completely understand it.

On the other hand, she was absolutely crazy out of her mind.

Engaged?

He'd been there, done that and his heart was far too raw to be considering that kind of commitment again. Even if it was only make-believe.

"Think about it," Gracie urged, drawing closer and placing a pleading hand upon his arm.

"I am," he said, his voice low and scratchy. He turned away from her, brushing her hand away from his arm. "And I think it's a bad idea."

"Only because you haven't thought it through," she countered crisply, linking her arm through his as if nothing was wrong, as if he hadn't just brushed her off. "Now that *I* think about it, this really would be a good thing for both of us."

"How's that?" he asked warily, wondering if he should even broach the subject with her. He was beginning to think too much information was a bad thing, and that maybe he was better off not knowing.

"Isn't it obvious?" She was getting animated now, both in movement and inflection. That put Kyle even more on edge.

"Not particularly."

"For you, it is the opportunity to enjoy your summer worry-free. You and I enjoy spending time together anyway, and this way you won't be bothered by Chelsea Daniels anymore. Once she believes you're engaged to another woman, you'll be free to roam about the town without any hassle. Do you see?"

Kyle stroked his chin. "Well, there is that." But that single advantage was hardly reason enough to get engaged, even if the *engagement* was only make-believe and temporary.

But this wasn't about him. It was really about Gracie. "And for you?"

Gracie pinched her lips together and looked away, her gaze distant. For a moment, she was silent. And then, so quietly Kyle had to lean in to hear her, she said, "I should think that would be obvious."

Kyle turned her around by the shoulders so he could look into her eyes. He needed to see what she was feeling. "Spell it out for me, Gracie. Why do you want me to do this thing? Why can't we just go back in there and tell your parents it was a misunderstanding? That I care about you, but that you are my friend?"

She pinned him with a green-eyed glare. "We can do that. Sure we can. And then I can go right back to life in the middle of nowhere. Doing nothing that really counts in the world. Whatever you want, Kyle."

So that was what this was about.

"You think being engaged to me will help you get out of Safe Harbor?"

She nodded voraciously, her smile tentatively returning. "It makes sense, doesn't it?"

It didn't, but he let her continue.

"The thing is, up to this point, I've never had a reason to go. But there were always reasons to stay, so I've stayed. But if I'm working through the pain of a broken engagement to you, I might just be given the opportunity to get away, to find a life outside Safe Harbor.''

''Do you really believe that?'' He was skeptical. For one thing, Gracie, having been born and raised here, couldn't appreciate Safe Harbor for what it was—well, a *Safe Harbor*.

More to the point, she couldn't comprehend the wonderful contribution she made to the society in this small part of the world. Safe Harbor without Gracie Adams would be losing something vital. She added a style and flair all her own to the place.

But she wanted to leave. She wanted to save the whole, big, wide world.

She might be an adult, but she had the vision of a child. She was naive in the best sense of the word.

And if she wasn't careful, if she didn't watch where she was going and what she was doing, she was going to get hurt.

Kyle wanted to protect her from all that. It was a deep, gut feeling he couldn't shake off, and he couldn't downplay.

The only problem was, he didn't have the slightest idea how to go about protecting Gracie. Did he brush her off and hope, by his rejection, she would live, learn and grow up a little?

Or did he take her on, and embrace this whole crazy scheme?

It wasn't a *bad* idea, as ideas went. Rather clever, in fact, now that he thought about it.

And it *would* get Chelsea off his back. He could

enjoy his summer *and* spend quality time with Gracie, which he wanted to do anyway.

He was being handed the perfect summer on a platter, and all he had to do was pick it up.

Could it get any better than that?

Gracie was pacing, and still twirling her hair around her finger. Occasionally she muttered something low and unintelligible under her breath. She sent him an occasional fleeting look, but steadfastly refused to meet his eyes.

"Gracie, stop pacing. You're going to wear a hole in the lawn," he teased dryly, shaking his head at her nervous movement.

"You're sounding like my father again," she groused, but she stopped moving and directed her gaze at him. It was an improvement.

"Come here," he said, holding out his arms to her, wanting with his whole heart to wrap a cloak of protection around her in the same way his arms wrapped around her small shoulders. "I know I'm going to live to regret this," he said, tenderly kissing the top of her head, "but I wanted to give my new fiancée a hug before we go in to meet the parents."

She whooped and squeezed his waist, nearly taking the breath from him.

"Meet the firing squad," he continued in an exaggerated monotone.

"Oh, stop," she said, swatting at him playfully. "It won't be all bad. I promise you that. This will be one summer you will *never* forget."

Chapter Six

Gracie climbed over a pile of ropes that smelled like raw fish. It wasn't a pleasant odor, and as she glanced back, she noticed Kyle had a hand over his mouth and nose.

Gracie herself had been down to the docks so many times she was used to it, and hardly noticed the unpleasant odors of fish and unwashed bodies. It was a requisite part of her service here, and she resolutely accepted it without wavering.

Once, the clapboard houses lining the dock had belonged primarily to the fishermen who made their living on the lake, but now there were few real fisherfolk in Safe Harbor. The trade had nearly disappeared here, as elsewhere, though ironically, the smell of raw fish still permeated the dock, a constant reminder to everything that was past.

The run-down shacks that had once belonged to

fishers' wives waiting for their husbands to return
from the sea, had now been turned into government-
run, low-income housing units, inhabited primarily
by destitute single mothers struggling to raise families on their own. These children ran and played
barefooted through the roughly paved streets, while
their grandmothers rocked and kept quiet watch in
squeaky chairs on rickety front porches that desperately needed a fresh coat of paint.

But there was one point in which these two cul-
tures, different in so many ways, converged.

The towering, steadfast lighthouse that stood
watch over them.

Gracie knew it was not a mistake that the best
view of the majestic lighthouse that gave Safe
Harbor its name was in its poorest district. The beam
of light, of hope, that shone from the tall, white
lighthouse was a message straight from God
above—light shining into the darkness.

And anything Gracie could do to help that message along, she would do. She was committed to
that, to these people.

And now she had Kyle alongside to help her in
her mission. *Dr.* Kyle, who would be a great help
in dispensing medical advice and treatment.

At the moment, he was her *fiancé* Kyle.

She wasn't sure she'd ever get used to calling him
that. She still wasn't sure how she'd gotten herself
into this mess in the first place.

But it had seemed like a good idea at the time,
she mused.

She felt guilty every time someone in town congratulated her about their *engagement,* especially since everyone seemed so sincerely happy about the good news. Chelsea, of course, hadn't been happy about it, but as Gracie had predicted, the fickle woman had quickly moved on to gamer territory— to one of the local boys who would pay her plenty of attention and soothe her shallowly wounded ego.

No permanent harm done, except the guilt she felt at deceiving people she cared about. And there was some good to come out of the feigned relationship Gracie shared with the handsome doctor. She had to admit it felt pretty good to be showing Kyle the part of her life that really meant something to her, something she shared with no one else.

She somehow knew that he would understand better than anyone what she was trying to do down at the docks, the difference she was trying to make in the lives of these people.

It almost felt *real.*

And there was the danger.

Because she hadn't expected *real* to feel so good, so right.

"Tell me again what we're doing down here," Kyle said, coming up behind her and resting his hands on her shoulders. His backpack, like hers, was chock-full of food and medical supplies, but his hands were free, and he massaged her shoulders gently around the shoulders of her own pack.

"I've already told you a hundred times," she said, exaggerating a sigh. "I don't have a plan, exactly. I just come down with my pack, some fresh fruit or whatever else I can think of at the time, and just go. Walk around. Talk to people. Interact. You know, mix with the locals. And then I see what comes of it.''

''Mmm,'' he said, close to her ear, as if he were only half paying attention.

''Kyle,'' she warned, her voice turning serious. ''They can't think you're there to give out charity, or they'll push you out of their district so fast your head will spin.''

He spun her around with his hands so she was facing him. Cocking his head to one side, he tipped up her chin with his knuckle. He stared at her for a moment before speaking. ''Gracie, not to state the obvious or anything, but you *are* giving them charity.''

Gracie frowned, feeling defensive. ''I know that, and they know that. But the moment I make them *feel* that way, I'm out of there.''

She saw him raise his dark eyebrows. To his credit, he looked genuinely interested in what she was saying. ''Why is that?''

''You have to understand where these people are coming from. They have to humble themselves enough in this life, taking food and housing from the government, and who knows what all else. They are as proud as you and I. Think about how you would feel if you couldn't provide bread for your children. If you had to take handouts from someone feeling philanthropic. How would you feel if you were in their shoes?"

She could see a muscle working in his jaw, and knew he was thinking about it. Here was a man who'd devoted his entire life to a service industry, to helping people get well.

Gracie already knew where his heart was. That's why she brought him down here.

"Let me just see if I get this straight," Kyle said as they walked down the first busy street in the dock district.

A makeshift game of baseball was being played by a ragamuffin lot of kids. A few of the boys had torn off their shirts to use as bases, and an old stick was quite effective as a bat. The only genuine piece of equipment they had was an old baseball, which the pitcher, a middle-grade girl with a backward-turned baseball cap, threw with surprising strength and accuracy.

Kyle tossed his backpack to the ground and pulled out some fresh oranges. He didn't immediately hand them out, though, as Gracie would have expected he might.

Instead, he took a deep whiff of one, held it in the air so everyone could see, then began juggling three in the air at a time.

The ball game stopped as the kids began gathering around Kyle, watching as he tossed one orange behind his back without missing a beat with the other two flying in the air. Then he flipped one or-

ange under his knee at a time, and under the other
knee, all without dropping a single fruit.

Suddenly he reached into the bag and grabbed
another, and then another, until he was juggling five
pieces of fruit in the air. The children were mes-
merized, and were flocked around Kyle as if he were
the Pied Piper playing a tune.

When he called on one boy to catch an orange
and then a nearby girl to catch another, there was
cheering and shouting; soon Kyle had made sure
each of the children was munching on a piece of
fresh fruit, and without insulting a single child's dignity.

When he winked at Gracie and zipped up his now
half-empty backpack, her heart welled up into her
throat. He really was magnificent.

"Am I catching on, or what?" he asked casually,
motioning her ahead of him.

"I think you've got it," she said dryly, walking
down the lane so he wouldn't see her true emotions.
"If you charm Mrs. Baske like you've charmed
these children, I'm going to be completely out of a
job. Then I'm really going to have to leave Safe
Harbor."

"Never," he assured her, stepping up beside her
and taking her hand, a gesture that was as oddly
reassuring as it was unnerving. He walked in silence
for a moment, gently swinging her hand, and then
added as an aside, "Who is Mrs. Baske?"

"You'll see," she said secretively. "We're going
to her house now."

Kyle didn't say anything else until they reached the rickety front porch, painted a faded yellow, that belonged to old Mrs. Baske. "She has been a widow for over a decade," Gracie explained quietly as she knocked on the screen door. "She dearly loved her husband, but she had no children, and now she lives here alone."

When Mrs. Baske called out, Gracie swept in the door, gesturing for Kyle to follow. He stepped in, noting that the screen door was tilted on its hinges, direly in need of repair.

Without preamble, Gracie moved into the kitchen and started a pot of tea, arranging cookies from her pack as delicately as possible on a flowery paper plate. It was the best she could do under the circumstances. Mrs. Baske did enjoy her tea.

When the kettle shrieked with steam, Gracie steeped the tea and filled three chipped and cracking china cups she found in the cupboard. Kyle helped her carry everything in to where Mrs. Baske sat in the living room, resting in an easy chair, with her feet propped on an old, worn ottoman. A large, fluffy orange cat lay across her lap, sleeping.

Mrs. Baske was the plump, grandmotherly type of woman Gracie remembered her own Grandma Adams being before she'd passed away when Gracie was a girl. She had salt-and-pepper hair that still retained much of its original black color. Mrs. Baske wore it swirled into a bun that accentuated her gray eyes, which still sparkled with life and laughter despite the trouble she'd seen in her long lifetime.

"My, my," exclaimed Mrs. Baske, putting a palm to her chest. "Who is this handsome fellow?" She gestured toward Kyle, who nodded in greeting. "Gracie, he nearly takes my breath clean away!"

Gracie knew her eyes were shining as she beamed at Kyle. "Doesn't he, though," she said wryly, inwardly agreeing with Mrs. Baske one hundred percent. Kyle's good looks and charm did tend to have that affect on women—of any age.

"I'm Dr. Kyle Hart, ma'am, at your service," he said, tipping the imaginary cowboy hat he'd left at home that day. "I'm happy to meet you."

"Likewise, I'm sure," said Mrs. Baske, laughing herself into a coughing fit. She hunched over and wheezed for a moment, clutching at her throat until she could catch her breath again.

Gracie moved to her side and put an arm around the old woman's frail shoulders, speaking softly to her in reassuring tones.

"Kyle's helping out Dr. McGuire. They're old friends from medical school. Wendy McGuire's almost due to have her baby soon, you know?" While Gracie talked, she nonchalantly took Mrs. Baske's pulse and slid her arm into a blood pressure cuff.

"I'd heard," Mrs. Baske said. "What does that make now, ten children for her?"

Kyle guffawed. "Only three. Two boys and a blessing."

Mrs. Baske beamed with delight and patted Kyle condescendingly on the cheek. "What a lovely way to phrase it, dear."

Gracie slipped her stethoscope into her ears and listened carefully to Mrs. Baske's heart and lungs. Mrs. Baske continued to entertain Kyle with her simple chattering and fascinating stories as Gracie continued her unobtrusive checkup.

"So, did you and Gracie meet at the clinic?" she asked, sending Gracie a look that she could not possibly mistake in meaning. When Mrs. Baske winked slyly, Gracie nearly choked in mortification.

Gracie could feel herself blushing hotly at the implications of what was being said, and what was being said between the lines. And even more that there were no longer any easy answers to the questions posed. Or maybe the answers were easy but the repercussions were complicated.

Either way, she was as confused as she'd ever been in her life.

"We met at the clinic," Kyle conceded with a smile in Gracie's direction. His eyes were gleaming with amusement as he slid a hand along his jaw to hide his smile. "To tell the truth, Mrs. Baske, Gracie asked me to run away with her."

"Did she, now?"

"Yes, ma'am, she did."

"And what did you say?"

Kyle's grin widened to epic proportions. "Why, I said yes, of course."

His gaze locked with Gracie's. "A man would have to be crazy not to take Gracie Adams up on an offer like that. And I've never been called crazy, whatever else I may have been called."

Mrs. Baske chuckled and held a delicate hand to her chest. "Truly?"

Kyle nodded. "Cross my heart," he said, making an *X* on his chest with his index finger. "Should we tell her, Gracie?"

The look he shot Gracie was one of amusement and tolerance, but all she felt was mortification and a very great sense of denial, not to mention the anger she felt at Kyle.

She wanted to shout at him to quit this silly game, to keep his mouth closed and the secret hidden, but she knew it wasn't Kyle who was in the wrong here.

She had started this facade, and it was up to her to keep it going.

And she had good reason. She just had to remind herself of that reason.

She had to remember what she was doing and why she was doing it. She had to remember the mission fields abroad that needed her services, and that Kyle was her ticket out of Safe Harbor.

She turned to the old woman and took a deep breath, grasping for courage to continue. "Mrs. Baske, we'd like you to be one of the first to know that we're engaged to be married."

Somehow, she managed to choke out the words. Lying wasn't her style, especially not to a sweet old woman like Mrs. Baske, who appeared utterly delighted by her announcement, clapping her hands and hooting in sheer delight.

"I knew it the moment you two walked in the door," she pronounced, taking Gracie's hand, then

Kyle's, and then placing them together across her lap. "Sometimes I just know about these things. I could see right away you were meant for each other."

If Gracie could have crawled into a hole and covered herself up with a big rock, she would have; but instead she forced herself to accept the voracious peck on the cheek Kyle offered as proof of his dedication to their future union, and the goodwill wishes Mrs. Baske continued to extend in a loud and scratchy voice.

Somehow, she forced herself to smile.

She couldn't fathom how Kyle was taking all this so easily, but he seemed completely at ease with his role as her fiancé. Every touch, every look, was completely in keeping with a man in love.

Apparently, the idea of the two of them being engaged was a good one, or at least *he* thought so. He'd obviously warmed to the idea.

At least that made one of them. The more she thought about it, the less she liked what she had done, and the less sure of herself she was feeling.

She turned her mind back to her medical work with Mrs. Baske, afraid to dwell anymore on her circumstances and wanting to shift the attention away from herself and her engagement.

"Your heart and lungs sound great, Mrs. Baske," she said cheerfully, patting the old woman on the arm and kneeling beside her chair. "You're in really good shape for your age. But I did notice your blood pressure is up a little bit."

Mrs. Baske waved her off with wide arms and a huff of breath. Gracie allowed her to express her dignity and her pride, and didn't try to correct her natural tendency to wave away medical support. She knew she would feel the same way in Mrs. Baske's position, distrusting the institution.

"Have you been taking your medicines properly, and watching your diet?" Gracie asked the question softly, still rubbing the woman's arm. She didn't want to sound like she was ordering or nagging, especially after the lecture she'd given Kyle on intruding in these people's lives.

Still, as a medical expert, she was obligated to do what she could for Mrs. Baske, and right now that meant trying to get her high blood pressure under control by whatever means she had available to her. And though Mrs. Baske might balk at the idea, that included using her medical knowledge.

Kyle caught her eye and cocked his brow, silently reminding her that she wasn't supposed to be making this sound like charity.

She frowned at him. As if she didn't know what she was doing.

But the alternative was unquestionable. Surely he knew that.

Again, she reaffirmed her decision to do whatever was necessary. She would do whatever she could do for Mrs. Baske.

By whatever means.

Kyle took the blood pressure sleeve from Gracie and slowly and thoroughly reexamined Mrs. Baske with a doctor's gentle touch. As he worked, he spoke quietly about the people he'd met and the things he'd learned in his time in Safe Harbor.

He kept Mrs. Baske laughing and nodding at his humorous but accurate renditions of people and places around town. She hardly noticed as he moved around her, checking all her vital statistics and giving her as complete a workup as possible with the limited resources available to him.

He nodded discreetly at Gracie as he released the sleeve from the elderly woman's arm, letting her know by his nod and his gaze that he'd obtained the same results she had, but he didn't pause or falter in the story he was telling Mrs. Baske.

After they shared another laugh, Kyle paused, absently running his fingers through the tips of his thick hair, obviously figuring the best way to broach the subject of Mrs. Baske's condition. At last he spoke, breaking into a gentle smile and placing a reassuring hand on the old woman's shoulder.

"I tell you what, Mrs. B. I really enjoyed coming down to see your place. You've got a fine little house here, and I appreciate your hospitality."

The old woman grinned.

"But now," Kyle continued, "it's your turn to come see mine. I want to show you some of my hospitality."

"Meaning?" the old woman asked wryly.

Gracie laughed. Mrs. Baske might be eighty-seven, but she didn't miss a beat.

Kyle shrugged casually. "I'd like you to come

see me at the clinic for some simple blood work, okay?''

As casual as his attempt had been, he sounded just exactly like the doctor he was.

Gracie grazed him with a look, which he returned innocently.

I know what I'm doing, he communicated clearly with his golden gaze.

Gracie teasingly rolled her eyes at him, causing him to break into a grin.

She would have snorted out loud at his blatant overconfidence if it weren't for Mrs. Baske being in the room. He might think he was scoring a few points with the elderly woman, but what he was really doing was getting them both permanently uninvited from Mrs. Baske's house.

Maybe even kicked out of the house right now, and probably quite unceremoniously, too.

Right when she was beginning to think Kyle was getting it, he had proven beyond a doubt that he didn't get it at all.

''Will you be there, Dr. Hart?'' Mrs. Baske asked suddenly, almost coyly, tapping her weathered chin with her index finger.

Gracie squeaked in surprise, nearly jumping out of her chair and tipping her hot tea into her lap. She recovered in what she thought to be a little less than graceful manner, considering that Kyle was watching her carefully.

Kyle chuckled and shot Gracie a look that let her know he knew exactly what was going through her mind. Then he winked at Gracie and gave Mrs. Baske his best, charming, toothy grin.

"I'll tell you what. For you, Mrs. Baske, and only because I especially like you, I'll even come and pick you up. I'll even borrow Gracie's Focus so you don't have to ride in a big old truck."

He paused before going in for the proverbial kill. "How does next Thursday morning sound?"

Mrs. Baske still looked somewhat unconvinced and uncomfortable under the pressure as she looked from Kyle to Gracie and back, and yet there was the sense that she was wavering, that she was actually considering Kyle's over-the-top request.

Gracie thought it was practically a miracle that they weren't being flipped out on their ears simply for suggesting such a thing. It wasn't something Mrs. Baske would have heard from anyone else, other than the handsome, charming Dr. Kyle, who apparently knew the strength of his own assets.

"And who will be wielding the needle?" the old woman asked caustically. She wrapped her arms around herself as an almost unconscious way to shield herself from the very idea.

"I will," Gracie assured her, looking to Kyle for reinforcement.

"She's really quite exceptional," Kyle chipped in cheerfully.

Mrs. Baske laughed and shot him a pointed look. "Oh, I'm sure *you* think so. But you have to admit you're a little bit biased on this subject, Kyle.

You're about to marry the woman. The question is, can she hold a steady needle?''

There was laughter in her eyes, and Gracie knew she was simply the brunt of good-natured teasing. Which meant, of course, that she could tease back. "Oh, if you think I'm good with a needle, you ought to see me with a sword in my hand."

"If you fence with a foil anywhere near as well as you fence with words…" Kyle teased, holding up his hands in defense.

Gracie stood, daintily set her teacup and saucer aside, and then set herself in a fencer's posture. She pretended to lunge forward, spearing him in the heart with the end of her invisible blade.

He lifted both eyebrows. *"En garde!"* he said with a brisk nod. "I do believe you've stabbed me through the heart, fair lady."

She laughed at his silliness. "And don't you forget it."

Mrs. Baske howled with laughter. "Oh, you two! Okay, okay, you can come get me Thursday," she conceded merrily. "How can I not give in?"

"Excellent!" Kyle said, patting Mrs. Baske's shoulder. "I'll be right on time."

"Yes, I'm sure you will," Mrs. Baske said dryly. "But as for today, I think you have stayed long enough, don't you?"

Kyle sputtered but didn't answer, looking completely stunned.

Mrs. Baske laughed at having caught him off

guard. "I know you have others to visit. Have you been to see Genevieve Franco yet?"

Kyle shook his head, his jet-black hair washing over onto his forehead. He was still mute, and looking completely befuddled.

"She's getting bigger and bigger every day. I sure hope she's taking the prenatal vitamins you gave her. I hear such bad things in the news about birth defects and things."

"We'll check in on Genevieve," Gracie promised, giving the elderly woman a tender hug. "You need to worry about yourself. Eat right, and take all your medicine. Promise?"

Mrs. Baske reached out and snagged Gracie's fingers as she stood to leave, pulling Gracie back to face her. "You know what a blessing you are to this town, don't you, Gracie Adams?"

Gracie swallowed hard over the lump of emotion that had formed in her throat. She flashed a panicked glance at Kyle, who just beamed at her, his eyes shining. Her first instinct was to shake her head, to deny Mrs. Baske's fervent words.

But the old woman never gave her the chance. Mrs. Baske turned to Kyle, coaxing him to her side of the fence. "She doesn't believe me, Doctor. What are we going to do about that?"

Kyle moved to Gracie's side, put an arm around her, and pulled her close to his chest. "Well, Mrs. Baske, we're just going to have to work together to prove to my *future wife* just how very much she's needed around here, aren't we, now?"

Mrs. Baske grinned, showing a full array of brown, crooked teeth. "Indeed, we will, Dr. Hart. Indeed, we will."

Kyle tossed his black Stetson across the room, not really caring that he didn't quite make the hat stand with his throw. Grunting wearily, he slumped into the nearest armchair and kicked up his feet, yanking at his cowboy boots one by one, and tossing each one across the room when he pulled it off his foot.

It had been a busy day, but not any more than the usual.

The truth wouldn't let him rest. Not even if he closed his eyes and feigned sleep.

It wasn't his work making him feel this way. He wasn't kidding anyone, including himself, by pretending otherwise.

As much as he loved what he did at the clinic, it couldn't make him feel tired and elated at the same time, charmed beyond reason and frustrated out of his mind so that he didn't know up from down, red from black. He was so confused he hardly knew the difference between sweet, sour and salty.

Only a woman could do that to a man.

In his case, it was one woman in particular. A redheaded, energetic bundle of trouble.

Gracie faced him off with her unique brand of talkative individuality he simply could not ignore, not even when he tried. She forced him to have emotions he could not afford to feel.

He pushed his palms against his eyes, straining against the throbbing pain. He didn't want this.

He wasn't ready to feel anything about anyone other than his wife. He hadn't come to Safe Harbor seeking new love—he'd come to be left alone.

He thought he'd be alone for the rest of his life. When he had married Melody, he'd never thought he'd love anyone in his whole life but her, and when he lost her, he'd thought he'd never love again.

And yet he knew in his heart that of all people, Melody wouldn't want him to be agonizing this way. She wouldn't want him to be grieving.

She'd want him to be living.

He just didn't know if he could.

At first he'd thought he'd made a big mistake, letting Gracie talk him into such an outrageous scheme as posing as her future husband. He'd actually thought the whole idea was crazy from the get-go.

The only reason he'd capitulated in the end was because she'd looked so sweet and helpless standing there, telling him about her overbearing parents, and about this being her only possible opportunity to get out of Safe Harbor.

It wasn't true, of course.

If Gracie would just open up her eyes and take a good look, she would realize that she was free to do whatever she wanted, up to and including leaving Safe Harbor for greener pastures. There was nothing holding her back, except herself.

And the most ironic thing of all was how very

much she was needed and wanted and *loved* right here in her hometown.

If only she could see it.

But in her mind, the only way out of her intolerable circumstances was to fake this engagement with him, so she had a legitimate reason—their eventual breakup at the end of the summer—to leave town.

Something all the people who depended on her would understand.

Something that would assuage her own guilty conscience.

And Kyle had felt sorry for her, gone along with her desperate pleas.

And he'd forced her to play the hand, too, when push came to shove. At Mrs. Baske's house, when it was time to admit they were engaged. Gracie had to face up to the fact that if this was going to happen, she was going to make it happen.

If she was going to do this, she was going to have to do it right.

He had to admit, though, that it wasn't all bad for him. He *was* getting something out of this unusual bargain. For one thing, Chelsea Daniels wasn't hanging all over him anymore, now that word had gotten out that he was otherwise spoken for.

And if the truth be told, the best part was that he got to spend extra time with Gracie. In fact, it was an outright requirement, not that anyone had to twist his arm to make him say uncle.

He couldn't get enough time with the incomparable Gracie Adams. The woman made him laugh out loud with her whacked-out sense of humor, and made his heart flip over with every glimpse of her outrageous hair and her glimmering eyes.

He shifted, sinking deeper into his easy chair with a contented groan. He stared without seeing, a half smile on his lips.

Gracie.

Gracie, who without consciously thinking about it, automatically put everyone else's needs above her own, who reached out to anyone and everyone within the range of her influence, be it to dole out medical help, or to dispense that quirky brand of spiritual wisdom she inherently possessed and readily shared.

To Gracie, Jesus was a real person, a relationship, and she communicated that extraordinary, supernatural connection wherever she went. She didn't practice her religion, she lived it.

And she had absolutely no idea how extraordinary she was, or how much people here in Safe Harbor depended on her.

If anyone could help him regain his equilibrium, show him the world and how to live life once again, it would be Gracie Adams.

But he didn't know if that was possible. He could only wait and see.

And pray.

Chapter Seven

"Gracie, are you sure you wouldn't rather be going to a movie? Or at least out to dinner at The Bistro, or something more romantic than…*this.*"

Gracie pushed back from the shelf of the hardware store, which also doubled as the auto parts store, having a small section of the back corner stocked with motor oil and antifreeze.

She had been searching through oil filter boxes, mumbling under her breath about the lack of selection of proper parts in Safe Harbor. How was a person supposed to keep an engine in working condition with such little inventory as this?

"Don't normal engaged couples tend toward more romantic activities on Friday evenings?" Kyle asked, brushing his fingers through the light black curls on his neck and distracting Gracie entirely from what she was doing.

She tried to meet his gaze, to keep her mind on her work, but Kyle wasn't looking at her at all. Or rather, he wasn't looking at her eyes. He was staring at her left cheekbone.

She shifted, refusing the urge to reach up and touch the spot he was staring at. Did she have a huge blemish so obvious he couldn't help but stare?

She decided to change the subject, or at least address the subject he'd brought up earlier. Movies and dinner and all that dating fluff. Locking her wrists behind her, she took a step toward him, closing the distance between them.

"We aren't exactly a *normal* engaged couple, now, are we?" she asked wryly, her voice catching on the words as she realized the truth in what she said.

Kyle chuckled, his throat sounding dry. "You can say that again. The two of us definitely defy all the bounds of normalcy."

He reached out a hand, gently stroking her cheek. When he was satisfied, he held up his index finger, which was blackened with grease. "Who wants to be normal?" he asked quietly. "We're...special."

She made a sound that was suspiciously like a snort. "We're...*something.*"

He lifted an eyebrow, and she shrugged.

"So, are we going to get your truck fixed tonight, or what?" she asked a little too brightly, turning away and breaking eye contact.

He grinned. "You're the grease monkey. I'm just along for the ride."

Gracie continued to astonish Kyle with her hidden abilities and diverse interests. Like tinkering with cars, as a prime example. She could change the oil, flush the transmission and the radiator and change all four spark plugs. Not to mention change a tire, and probably align the things, too, if she had the time and the proper equipment.

Until this year, Kyle had made a habit of bringing his truck to the dealership to get serviced. Sure, he was able to check his own oil, but he didn't think he could tell a spark plug wire from a fuel line to save his life.

Now, though, the nearest dealership was miles away, so Kyle had originally planned to visit the local Safe Harbor garage for his service work.

Gracie wouldn't hear of it.

She informed him, in that way she had of looking both offended and embarrassed at the same time, that she was quite capable of servicing his truck. Moreover, she would do it for nothing. As a friend.

And the really amazing thing was that she was capable of doing it. Gracie wasn't just a respectable grease monkey, either—Kyle thought she was good enough to go into business with it if she wanted to, and give the shop around the corner some competition.

But of course, her interest extended only to helping her friends—without expecting a dime for her services, all from the goodness of her heart. Her naturally openhanded personality always managed to take him by surprise, even though he spent nearly all his free time now with her, studying her. He sometimes felt he was getting to know the real woman behind those gorgeous green eyes and sunny smile.

"Tell me again why you know how to change the oil in my truck?" he asked, barely thinking about it as he brushed his hand down the soft, silky length of her red hair. He loved it when she wore it down long, untethered by a ponytail or barrette.

She turned to him, placed a hand still holding a box containing an oil filter on her hip and cocked her head to one side. "Would you be asking me this question if I were a man?"

His gaze widened and he swallowed hard. Kyle took a mental step backward as his mind spun with the impact of her words.

Her tone had been quiet and nonaccusatory, which in itself wasn't exactly Gracie's usual style. He realized she was merely showing him the error of his ways in the most polite way possible. For Gracie, anyway. So that he could save face if he wanted to and give her a good, healthy argument.

But he wasn't going to do that.

"No, I don't suppose I would," he admitted, choking back the nominal burst of pride that rose to halt his words. "But I didn't mean the question as an insult. Honestly."

Gracie laughed, the buoyant sound a balm to his soul. "I know. You're a lot of things, Hart, but a chauvinist you are not. In fact, I'd have to say you're the most gentlemanly man I have ever met."

Kyle screwed his mouth up in half a smile. "Thank you. I think." He chuckled. "What can I say? I had to ask what a beautiful woman like you was doing in a place like this. Especially on a Friday night, which is—and I have this on good authority— Safe Harbor date night." He held up a quart of oil and waved it at her.

Gracie was quiet for a long moment, neither speaking nor moving. Finally she shrugged. "Somebody's got to do it," she said crisply, as if that explained everything.

"Is that your motto?" he teased.

She looked at him, surprised. "Maybe. But then again, maybe it's just my defense mechanism."

She seared him with a grin.

Kyle frowned, trying to look serious, but he knew the mirth in his eyes was giving him away. "I can see that about you."

She jolted toward him, her eyes wide, clearly not sure what to make of his comment. Her expression kept changing as she covered the possibilities—that he was serious, teasing or who knew what else?

He reached for her shoulders and rubbed his palms down her arms. "I'm kidding, Gracie."

He felt rather than saw her relax. "I have to poke fun at you. I can't help myself." He chuckled loudly when she tensed once again. This time he knew the tension wasn't inward. It was directed at him.

"I'm glad I amuse you," she said in a tight voice, scowling. Kyle would have been concerned, except he could hear the laughter in her voice.

"Well, Ms. Somebody's Got To Do It, my truck is still waiting," he reminded her, pulling out a wad of bills to pay for the car parts.

Gracie didn't argue. Kyle grinned, his stomach fuzzy with this crazy feeling he'd won some kind of battle. He grinned and shook it off.

Feeling emboldened as they left the hardware store, Kyle held his hand out to her, palm up. He'd wanted to ask before, but hadn't known how. He felt funny any other way. And it wasn't chauvinism. It was just one of those guy things.

Gracie narrowed her eyes on him, clearly suspicious. "What?"

"I'll drive," he said casually, though he knew his voice sounded tight. "The keys?"

"It's my car."

Kyle winked at her and dropped his hand to his side. "Right. Sorry."

"Oh, all right," she said with a deep, dramatic sigh as she dug around inside her purse for her keys. "I really don't care if you drive my car."

Kyle shrugged as if it didn't matter to him one way or the other. "I just thought it would make us look more—oh, I don't know—*engaged*. That's all."

"You just like to drive, and you know it."

"That, too." Kyle grinned and nodded.

She elbowed him playfully and slipped the keys into his palm.

Kyle tightened his fist around the keys. Somehow he knew instinctively something bigger had just happened between them than Gracie merely handing over her car keys.

Could it be possible she was finally starting to trust him?

He grinned as he accompanied Gracie to the passenger side of her little blue hatchback and opened the door for her.

He was moving around to the driver's side when Gracie popped back out of the car, leaning her elbows on the hood and drawing Kyle's full attention.

Kyle lifted his eyebrows, waiting to see what had Gracie's attention.

"Is that Constance over there?" Gracie flicked her chin in the general direction of the street. Down the street, to be precise.

For a Friday evening date night, the streets around the square could hardly be called crowded, and Kyle immediately spotted what Gracie was referring to— or rather, whom.

Constance, her big old Cadillac parked at an awkward angle against the curb, was stomping around her vehicle and, it seemed from Kyle's perspective, landing any number of blows on it. He could only imagine the words that were being added to the altercation, and he bit back a grin, knowing Gracie might misinterpret.

"Oh, my," Gracie said aloud.

"I don't think that's what Constance is saying," Kyle muttered under his breath.

"Kyle Hart! You rascal."

He shrugged. She was probably right on that account.

"We have to go help her."

"Sure. Yeah. Of course we do." He'd spent his whole life keeping his nose *out* of other people's business, but in the short time he'd known Gracie, he'd learned a whole new way of looking at things.

People really did need help sometimes. And what's more, they often wanted it.

Of course, he hadn't a clue what he was going to do in order to help a fuming Constance out with her apparently uncooperative Caddy. Unless maybe it was to grab a baseball bat and finish the job Constance had started with her fist.

He shoved his hands into his pockets and whistled as he followed Gracie to where her friends were. Justine Clemens, Elizabeth Neal and two other League women Kyle would have classified as past middle age but nowhere near elderly poured out of the car, groaning at the problem and laughing at Constance's reaction. Finally a red-faced Nathan stepped from the passenger side of the car shrugging when Kyle chuckled and lifted an eyebrow.

"What can I say?" Nathan mumbled amicably. "I like a pretty face."

"They appear to like you, too," Kyle said, giving his friend a tough-guy nudge.

"Like I said," Nathan said again. "What can I say?"

"I'd say I want to know your secret," Kyle said

smoothly, "but at this point I'm not sure that I really want to know."

Nathan nodded at Gracie. "You only need one."

Kyle hooted with laughter. "Yeah. Especially that one. She keeps me busy enough for ten women. I can't even imagine a carful."

"You've got quite a carload in there," Gracie said, walking over and obviously catching the tail end of the conversation. At least, Kyle hoped she'd caught only the tail end and not the whole thing. "Where are all of you off to, tonight?"

"Town hall," offered Elizabeth, fanning herself with what looked like an old church bulletin.

Gracie looked stunned, though Kyle couldn't imagine why.

"Haven't you heard?" Justine asked gently, her gaze straying to Nathan for just the slightest moment before she continued. "Chief Creasy has called a public meeting. Apparently he wants to make some kind of public announcement."

Kyle cringed inwardly, though he didn't make any outward appearance that the words meant anything to him. Every person standing on this sidewalk knew what kind of exhibition was being played out, and why. And who it involved.

He suddenly felt as if he was standing on a sidewalk of eggshells.

Gracie had been standing equally frozen, her expression moving from stunned to contemplative. Suddenly she bolted into action, moving to Constance's side.

"So that's what it is," she murmured, her voice low and carrying only far enough for Kyle to hear.

She smoothed back her hair with her palm and stepped into the fray, grasping Constance firmly by the shoulders and leading her away from the car—or at least out of kicking range.

"Constance, you need to take a break," Gracie coaxed, rubbing her hand across her friend's back. "If you keep this up, you're likely to break something here. And it's probably going to be one of your bones."

Constance looked at her with wide, startled eyes, and then hiccuped a laugh.

"Neither Dr. Hart or myself are on call tonight, nor do we wish to be called in on a special emergency. So do us both a favor, not to mention poor Millie, and stop beating up on the poor old girl."

Again Constance chuckled. "Gracie, you are the only one who remembers that my car has a name. Joseph, may he rest in peace, thought I was out of my mind naming my car, but she just seemed like a Millie to me."

"And she would prefer to remain without dents, thank you very much."

Constance sighed. "I suppose I'm going to miss the meeting now. Maybe it's just as well. I've been stressed about it ever since I heard."

Kyle walked up and draped his arm around Gracie's shoulders. "What time is the meeting?"

"Eight o'clock."

Kyle looked down at Gracie with a questioning look. "It's seven forty-five."

"We can walk from here, but we may be a few minutes late," Justine said.

"Not me," said Elizabeth. "These old knees won't make it a block, not even with the help of both these handsome gentlemen."

Gracie already had the hood of the car open, and was turning the key in the ignition.

"We'll be there in time," she assured everyone. "It's merely a dead battery. I have jumper cables in my car. Let me pull it around."

Kyle didn't have time to think about the fact that it was Gracie coming to the rescue and not him this time. Gracie's friends were putting to good use the time they had to wait for the car to be fixed—and it involved Kyle.

"She's quite a woman, that Gracie," said Elizabeth in a crackled old voice.

Justine smiled, catching the drift. "The kind of woman any man would be lucky to marry."

"Uh, sure," Kyle agreed, wishing despite the fine weather that he had a great big coat he could wrap around himself, including his head.

Especially his head.

"You know, I knew Gracie when she was a babe in diapers," said Barbara, a longtime League member. "I watched her grow up from just a little sprite. Why, I remember when she took the Lord into her heart. Blessed little thing. She was only four years old. But she knew what she was saying, mind you. Her heart was changed for the good of God.''

"Wow,'' said Justine. "What a special moment to remember. Kyle, were you a cradle Christian, or do you remember a specific date and time God called you to Himself?''

Kyle shifted from foot to foot, jamming his fingers through his hair and looking from woman to woman, then to Nathan for help, though he quickly realized no help was forthcoming from that end. Even Nathan was full of curiosity about him.

And he didn't want to talk about himself.

"It's the type of question we'll go over in premarital counseling,'' Justine suggested offhandedly, as if that information would make speaking now any easier. "When would be the best time for the three of us to get together, by the way? We need to meet once a week.''

Premarital counseling? He practically choked on the words. Were he and Gracie going to have to go that far to make this charade work?

"I...uh...med school,'' he said at last, then clamped his mouth closed, unwilling and perhaps unable to say any more on the subject.

He didn't want to tell them that Melody had found the love of Christ first, and then had oh-so-gently shown him what it meant to be a Christian.

He took a deep breath to steady himself. It was a tough memory. One he really couldn't handle right now.

Suddenly Gracie was by his side, her hand on his forearm.

"Are you okay?" she asked quietly.

He swallowed hard. "Yeah."

And he was. Now that Gracie was by his side, he would be okay.

"It's a lot faster if two people work the jumper cables," she said. "I could use your help."

"Let's see, negative to the positive and the—"

"No!" she protested.

He laughed loudly.

She shook her head. "You got me that time, Hart. I'm warning you, though. I get even."

"Did you know we have to go through premarital counseling?" he asked casually as he stuck his head under the hood of Gracie's car.

"Sure," she said. "But not right away. I don't think. Isn't that for, like, right before the big event?"

"Not to hear Justine tell it. She's trying to nail me down on a time."

"You're kidding."

Kyle snorted. "I wish I was. She wants to know everything about us. And I mean *everything*."

Gracie turned around. She stared at him for a moment, as if soaking up his emotion. She didn't look uncomfortable or threatened by the possibilities, as he was, but she did look concerned about him. "Don't worry. I'll get us out of it somehow. I won't put you in an embarrassing situation."

"It's not that, it's just—" he started, but Gracie cut him off with a look. She knew him too well.

"Get in the Caddy and rev her up, will you?" she asked, carefully inspecting the engine.

Kyle slipped behind the wheel, and thankfully, the car turned over immediately, followed by a loud cheer from the sidewalk. "Go, Gracie. Go, Gracie."

"Guys, please!" she protested.

Constance gave her a warm hug. "We'd invite you to come along with us in my car, but I'm afraid we have too many people in here already."

"I'm sure we'll be fine in mine," she assured them with a laugh.

"You can follow us," Nathan offered.

"They know where the town hall is, Nathan," Constance said, sounding like a mother hen. "Besides, they might have other plans. They're a young couple in love, though I'm not sure you don't ever remember that stage of your life," she teased flirtatiously.

Nathan's laugh sounded forced. "You'd be surprised, Constance. You'd be surprised."

"We'll see you at the hall," Kyle said, opening Gracie's door for her before slipping behind the wheel himself.

"How did you know I wanted to go to the meeting?" she asked suspiciously.

"Because, Gracie, you have an incurable need to know everything that goes on in Safe Harbor. Besides, the alternative is giving my truck an oil change. It's not much of a choice."

"Oh, Kyle, I'm sorry. With all the ruckus, I forgot all about your truck."

"It's okay. My truck will live. I haven't given it a name, so it doesn't experience the emotions latent in Constance's Cadillac."

Gracie clapped a hand over her mouth to smother her laugh. "Oh, Kyle. I promise I'll work on your truck tomorrow morning."

Kyle shrugged. "That will work for me, but don't go out of your way on my account. Whenever works for you will work for me."

He glanced toward her. "Besides, if the truth be told, I kind of want to go to this town meeting tonight, too."

"You do?" She sounded genuinely surprised, and he didn't know whether to feel amused or offended.

"Well, sure. A big-city fellow like me has never been to a small-town meeting," he said, taking on a fake accent. "I want to see what it's like so I can put it in my scrapbook."

"Boring, usually," she provided for him. "Now tell me why you really want to go."

He turned a corner and found a parking space on a side street near the town hall. From the look of things, everyone in town was here tonight.

Turning off the ignition, he gripped the steering wheel with his fists and turned to her. "I want to go," he said slowly, enunciating each word, "because I care about these people. I'm beginning to see the interrelationships that are going on here, and I want to be around—not just to observe, but to help.

This is a tough time for Safe Harbor, and for many people who live here.''

He pulled in a ragged breath. "I'm new, but maybe I'm here for a reason.''

Gracie launched herself across the seat and threw herself into his arms, nailing him with such a kiss that his head spun around dizzily, and he was glad he was sitting down.

"You are the sweetest, kindest man in the whole world,'' she told him earnestly. "And I'm glad we're engaged.''

He wondered if she remembered that their engagement was just a hoax. At the moment he didn't feel inclined to remind her.

They walked hand in hand into the town hall and sat near the back and to the side. Kyle suspected Gracie had chosen these seats so she could see not only what was going on up front but also what was happening in the audience.

There wasn't much of a wait. Chief Creasy was a prompt, organized man who believed in moving forward and doing his duty. He was tall, thin and balding slightly, but he had the bearing of a police officer, and there was no doubt from the harrowed lines crossing his face that he'd earned every year of service.

"Many of you have been speculating about my situation as police chief,'' he said without preamble when people quieted.

Gracie shot a wide-eyed glance at Kyle, who

slipped his arm around her and squeezed her reassuringly on the shoulder.

"First, let me thank you for all the wonderful years I've had here in Safe Harbor. I thank God for every one of them, and for every one of you."

There was a collective gasp as the meaning of his words penetrated through the room.

"Now, let me say change is inevitable. And often, change can be good. In this case, I think it is very good."

He paused to wipe his forehead with a handkerchief. "I'm here tonight to announce my early retirement."

A roar of disapproval met his words.

He held up his hands. "Please, people. Listen. I'm not retiring right away. I won't be leaving until the end of the summer. I just wanted you to know so it doesn't come as a complete surprise to you.

"I've already got an excellent replacement lined up, a young man named Matthew Trent from Green Bay. I'm sure he will be excellent in the job, and that you will give him the same caliber of support and enthusiasm you've always given me."

Kyle's gaze moved to Constance, who was tapping her foot rhythmically on the floor. Nathan sat beside her, shoulders square and feet planted solidly on the ground. But if Kyle didn't miss his guess, the man looked relieved. Kyle couldn't blame him.

Someone asked Chief Creasy what he would do with his retirement. A single man could get quite lonely, Kyle mused. But it sounded as if Charles had a lot on his plate—traveling and golf, and he was still going to be training men on the shooting range, as he was an expert marksman.

Gracie clutched Kyle's shirt. "It's because of Constance, isn't it?" she whispered raggedly. Kyle knew she was feeling this a lot more than he was. She'd spent her whole life in this town.

"I haven't a clue, Gracie. Maybe he just wants to do other things with his life besides work."

"You know that's not true."

Kyle shrugged and rubbed her fingers, which were still gripping his shirt. "Probably not. But God works out everything for the best, doesn't He?"

"It's hard to see sometimes," Gracie said, her voice gruff. "There's no way to make a happy ending for everyone when you've got two men and only one woman. I mean, I believe with my whole heart that Nathan and Constance have something special, but still…poor Charles."

"Gracie, you can't possibly make everything right in the world. It just isn't going to happen."

"That doesn't stop me from wanting it to happen."

Chief Creasy was being presented with an award for his service, so they stopped talking and supported him with their attention and their applause.

Afterward, to Kyle's surprise, the chief made a beeline for Constance and Nathan, shaking their hands and chatting comfortably with them. It seemed there was no ill will among the three.

As Kyle and Gracie stood, Gracie took Kyle's

hand and squeezed it hard. He smiled down at her, glad he could be with her on this difficult evening.

Suddenly, without warning, a feeling of happiness poured down on him like a warm summer rain. He couldn't imagine wanting to be anywhere else in the world than right here. Right now.

With the people of Safe Harbor.

And most of all, with Gracie.

Chapter Eight

The morning of July fourth dawned bright and cheery, with no sign of clouds to mar what looked to be a perfect day for a picnic. And in Safe Harbor, people knew how to picnic.

Kyle was up early, preparing a special wicker picnic basket for two, full of cold deli meats, cheeses and fruits. He'd spent the day before shopping for everything he needed, wanting to cut everything from the cheese to the melons fresh for himself.

He'd even bought a new red-checked cotton tablecloth for the occasion, with matching cloth napkins and little plastic napkin rings in the shape of roosters. He wanted to give Gracie something to *crow* about, he thought, holding back a grin.

After washing his hands in the bathroom sink, he looked in the mirror, assessing his black jeans and black T-shirt, black boots and black Stetson.

Well, at least he knew his colors matched, he thought wryly.

He couldn't believe how nervous he was about this community picnic, almost like a teenage boy on his first date. His getting all gussied up like a trussed chicken reminded him of another day, a day not that long in the past when he was staring in this very same mirror and wondering, just as he was now, where the day would take him. What the future would hold.

Memorial Day. The day of the infamous bachelor's block auction that he'd made such a muck of. The day he'd made a complete fool of himself, preening and primping before a bunch of women like he had no pride at all. The day Gracie Adams had saved his life by swinging out of a tree to bid on him.

He wouldn't be forgetting that anytime soon. It would definitely go down in infamy.

But then again, in a very real way, that day had brought him to Gracie, and he thought he might stand on any number of humiliating bachelor's blocks to make his way to her door.

He wondered, in passing, if she thought it was worth it.

Buying him, that is.

She'd certainly got her money's worth, and he wasn't talking about rototilling.

Wasn't he posing for her as her fiancé for the entire summer? Wasn't he providing her with the coveted *way out* she was longing for? Surely that was worth something to her.

It was worth something to him.

And today, he found himself looking forward to that same small-town community outing—that close-knit good-time feeling—that had once scared him to death. He couldn't believe he was actually *enjoying* the thought of a picnic with his friends and neighbors, with a flock of noisy children running and screaming underfoot and fireworks popping overhead.

What a difference a little over a month could make in a man's life. His thoughts and his feelings—his whole belief system, really—had changed so much in such a short time.

He'd certainly not been feeling light and giddy on Memorial Day, though the nervous swirling in the pit of his stomach might share some similar characteristics with what he was feeling today.

Today he wasn't anxious.

He was *anticipating*.

Kyle was thrown suddenly from his thoughts by a rapid, thunderous knock at the door. "You ready in there, cowboy?"

Kyle grinned. It was Wendy McGuire. She and Robert had insisted that Kyle and Gracie spend the day with them and their two boys at the park, but Kyle was still holding out for that picnic for two, knowing that Wendy, an incurable romantic herself, would understand his desire to be alone with Gracie.

Kyle adjusted his hat and headed for the door,

pausing only long enough to grab his picnic basket loaded full of goodies.

"Whaddaya got in there, Uncle Kyle?" Ben, the older boy, asked as soon as Kyle slid into the middle seat of the black Suburban. He wasn't technically related to the McGuire boys, of course, but Kyle had been a close friend of the family since before Ben was born. It had just seemed natural for him to develop into the role of an uncle when the boys were born. "Got any surprises for me and Bo?"

Kyle slid Gracie, who was seated beside him opposite the heavily laden basket, an amused look, then made a big show of peeking under the lid of the container. "I don't know, Ben," he said, slapping the lid closed, and then peeking once more under the lid. "Hmm. It looks like there might be *something* in here."

The six-year-old youngster perked right up, and four-year-old Bo was squirming in his car seat, trying to get a look at whatever it was Uncle Kyle was looking at in the basket.

Kyle put one hand tentatively into the basket and frowned in concentration as he felt back and forth around the bottom. "Oh, yeah, boys," he said, pinching his face into a big frown, "something's definitely squirming around in here."

Gracie stuck out her tongue and made a face, and Kyle barked out a laugh.

"Yeah. Something's wiggling. It's wiggling and wiggling and…"

He paused, widening his eyes as if in horror.

"It's—it's got my thumb. Oh, no! It's wrapped around my wrist."

He bulged his eyes out and twisted his mouth up. "It's…a *snake!*"

With that, he made a loud screeching noise that he belatedly thought might make Robert drive right off the road, and tossed the green rubber snake back at the giggling youngsters before they had a moment to figure out what he was going to do.

The boys both screamed so loud Kyle thought heaven probably heard the sound. Wendy glazed him with a look that gave him no doubt what she thought of his juvenile behavior, and Robert made a good deal of loud noise himself, telling everyone else to keep it down in the truck.

Kyle put his arm along the back of the seat and grinned cheekily at Wendy and Robert, feeling very pleased with himself.

Gracie swatted his shoulder with her palm. "How could you do that? That was so…"

"Boyish?" he supplied for her.

She stared at him for a moment or two, surprised, and then fought a smile. Finally, she burst into laughter. "Yes, I guess so. How awful you are, to torture those poor children that way!"

"I saw the snake in the general store the other day when I was browsing around, and I thought how much fun Ben and Bo would have with it. I remember how much I liked rubber snakes when I was a kid." He winked at Gracie. "Especially when I had the chance to frighten pretty girls with them."

Gracie gingerly patted the picnic basket between them, careful not to tip up the lid. The expression on her face was priceless, and Kyle held back his smile.

"Are there any more surprises in here I should worry about?" she asked, half tentatively, half clearly in challenge.

Kyle chuckled and shook his head. "There are surprises, Gracie. Something for you, even, if you behave yourself," he said with a wink. "But I don't think you need to be worried about these surprises."

"No snakes?"

"No snakes. I promise."

By this time they had reached the park, and the next few minutes were a virtual flurry of activity as they took out blankets and baskets, lawn chairs and coolers, and made their way slowly up the green, stopping to greet friends and neighbors as they went. Everyone was talking to everyone, and it was a whirlwind of friendly chaos in the park.

The young McGuire boys dashed up the green ahead of everyone, hollering and wrestling and rolling on the grass as they went. "C'mon, Uncle Kyle, we have to get up by the gazebo," Ben urged, pulling on his uncle's hand and urging him forward.

"Why is that, Ben?"

"You can see the fireworks best from the gazebo," Gracie supplied, coming up behind Kyle and putting her free arm around him. In her other arm she carried a box of plates and utensils, including long grilling forks. "Isn't that right, Ben?"

"Yeah! Yeah! Fireworks!" The boy agreed enthusiastically.

Suddenly he paused, hooked his index finger in his mouth, and surveyed Kyle and Gracie for a moment. "Uncle Kyle?"

"Yeah, buddy?"

"When you marry Gracie, then that will make her my Aunt Gracie, right?" he asked sloppily from around his finger.

Gracie looked stunned, so Kyle fielded the question, putting his hand on the young boy's shoulder. "Why, yes, Ben, I guess she would be your aunt."

"*Will* be your aunt," he corrected himself quickly, sliding a glance at Gracie, who still was standing beside him looking dumfounded. "Why do you ask?"

"Can I call her Aunt Gracie?"

It was an innocent enough question, but Gracie looked liked she'd swallowed a toad. Kyle didn't want to answer for her, but he wasn't at all sure she could answer for herself.

Her face was as red as her hair.

"Gracie?" he queried gently.

"I...um..." She faltered to a halt, then tried once again. "I guess that would be okay, Ben. If you want to."

"Aunt Gracie," Ben promptly responded, taking his finger out of his mouth and grinning as if he'd made some profound discovery.

Gracie made a choking sound.

Kyle took her elbow and headed her off toward

the trees, noting that it didn't take much effort to
lead her away. "Tell your mom and dad that Uncle
Kyle and *Aunt* Gracie went for a walk, okay Ben?"
he called over his shoulder.

"'Kay," the youngster agreed easily, and waved
at them as they walked away.

"Are you okay?" he whispered in Gracie's ear
just as they made the tree line. He slipped his arm
around her waist, ostensibly to better support her,
but mostly just because he liked the feeling of his
arm around her.

They were alone on this part of the wooded path,
but they were never really beyond the shadow of
being overheard, especially on a day like today
where everyone and their brother were promenading
around on the green.

"You look like you've seen a ghost."

"Did you hear what he said?" she said raggedly
in low undertones, her choked voice absolutely filled
with mortification. One hand clung to the fabric of
his shirt like a claw.

"Sure," Kyle said easily, rubbing her back with
his fingers, partially to get her to relax her grip on
his shirt. "He wants to call you Aunt Gracie. It's a
compliment, Gracie."

"Don't you think I know that?" she whispered
harshly, pulling him around to face her and digging
her other hand into his shirt fabric. She used her grip
to shake him just a little. "Don't you see where this
is going? It's completely out of hand."

Kyle placed his arms around her shoulders and

drew her close to his chest, where he could drop his head into her hair and inhale deeply, enjoying the fresh, fruity scent of her shampoo and the feel of her in his arms.

"Gracie, hon, this is exactly what you knew would happen."

"I just didn't think…"

"That the kids would take you seriously?" he finished for her. "Does it surprise you that no one sees through this ruse you and I have created? Have you stopped to wonder why?"

He felt her nod under his chin, though she didn't say anything. At least her breath was beginning to slow down and become more even.

"Because they want you to be happy, Gracie. They love you, and they want what's best for you. And for some unknown, crazy reason, they think that what's best for you is *me*."

She leaned back and looked up at him. "I wonder why that is?" The teasing glitter was back in her eyes, at least. Kyle was grateful for that.

Ignoring the desire to pull her tightly in his arms and kiss her until her eyes glowed with something other than amusement, he gave her a quick peck on her bottom lip and grabbed her hand, pulling her back toward the tree line and the green.

And the people.

Kyle didn't trust himself alone with her right now. Being alone with Gracie meant too many emotions for one man to handle. Better to be with a group of friends, where he could filter his feelings through the common sieve of community.

In the few minutes they'd been gone, the McGuires had been joined by several other families, many of whom he knew from church functions. Kyle recognized Constance and her little grandson Joey, Alex and Holly Wilkins, Russ and Annie, Nathan, Justine and Elizabeth.

Community.

Most of the Women's League, Kyle realized, was here in force. These ladies were the ones who were most supportive of his engagement to Gracie, who had encouraged her when she'd made her big announcement.

They were the same ones who would ride him out of town when they broke it off.

For some reason, that thought bothered him more than it used to, when he'd first thought about it. And not just that he would alienate people he'd grown to love and respect.

It had always been his intention to leave at the end of the summer. Wendy would have her baby, and Robert would be able to return to his full schedule at the clinic. Kyle was just filling in, after all.

When Wendy had her baby, he would no longer be needed in Safe Harbor.

He had a life in Houston in which to return. He had a neurological practice with a number of partners. They considered him on sabbatical.

He could return to his extravagant condo and all the things he'd worked so hard to attain.

He just didn't want to.

"Who wants hot dogs?" he called out, dropping Gracie's hand and striding into the crowd as if he could somehow lose himself in it. He tried not to look back at Gracie at all. "If Robert will get the grill lit, I'll do the honors."

But Gracie was right behind him all the way. There was a roar of approval as she presented Kyle with a black apron and hung it around his neck, reaching around him to tie the strings in back, and planting a big, noisy kiss on his cheek when she was done.

At least the apron was black, Kyle thought wryly, so he could continue on his black clothing theme of the day. On the front of the apron was a big, smiling pink pig and the words Pig Out in scratchy white letters.

Kyle obligingly picked up a long pair of tongs and waved them in the air, then went to work on grilling the hot dogs. It wasn't exactly gourmet cooking, but he sure didn't mind. The smell of the smoking grill, the surrounding evergreens, the sound of the children laughing and running, and adults talking and calling out to each other…

He was *happy*.

It was an astounding revelation.

He was really, truly happy. For this one moment in time, he could accept everything that was going on around him and be grateful for it.

For now, his past only served to make the present even more precious, more palatable. And his experiences in Houston, everything he'd learned in his life up to this moment, only served to make Safe Harbor seem more like Eden itself.

He'd made his share of mistakes. He'd focused too much on his medical career and not enough on his family, believing that provision of material things would make up for his lack of attention, for his very presence.

He'd loved. And he'd lost. He'd schmoozed his way through champagne and caviar and found, in the end, that hot dogs and potato chips were more to his liking.

From his vantage point at the grill, he could see Gracie deep in conversation with some of the ladies of the Women's League. From time to time she would look his way, send him a look or smile he knew was just for him. He wondered if she did it on purpose, or whether she unconsciously reached out to him with her gaze and her smile.

He had to watch himself. He was getting downright mushy in his old age. And more to the point with this tough-to-please Safe Harbor crowd, he was going to burn the hot dogs if he wasn't careful.

He'd just finished taking the last hot dog off the grill when suddenly there was a horrifying scream from the direction of the gazebo.

Everyone ran in every which direction. Chaos ruled as shouts rang out everywhere.

Kyle took a quick assessment of the situation, his medical training kicking in. He looked around carefully, noting the position and situation of each per-

son in the park. He immediately saw what was
wrong.

Little Joey, Constance Laughlin's one-and-a-half
year old grandson, who was visiting while his parents were away on a cruise, had apparently been
playing with a stick, swinging it back and forth over
by the old wooden gazebo, for though he was now
screaming, he still held the stick in his hands.

Joey had, Kyle surmised, hit a wasps' nest, and
the angry insects were buzzing everywhere about
him. The little boy was screaming, running and
throwing his arms around, swinging the stick as he
twirled away from the angry insects.

They were all actions, Kyle realized immediately,
the boy should not be doing in a swarm of wasps,
though of course he was too young to know that,
and too frightened to grasp the concepts even if he
was old enough to know better.

Kyle shifted into high gear, but before he could
get anywhere near the little boy, Nathan, dressed
only in khaki shorts and a tight white tank top that
left his arms and shoulders completely exposed, was
in the midst of the swarm, taking the little boy in
his arms, carefully shielding the boy's face with his
hands while he slowly but firmly removed himself
and the youngster from the swarm of wasps and
rolled them both as quickly as possible into the
nearby creek.

The creek contained barely enough water to cover
their ankles, let alone completely immerse them. But
Nathan faithfully rolled and splashed first the boy,

and then himself, until the swarm of angry wasps gave up and went elsewhere.

Kyle, practically scrambling on his hands and knees in his haste through the grass and gravel, reached the bank at the same time as Gracie, just as Nathan carried a quivering Joey out of the water.

Nathan didn't hesitate, but went straight to Gracie, who already had a bag open on the ground beside her and was spreading a wool blanket out on the ground for Joey to lie on.

Kyle quickly stepped up to help Nathan lay little Joey gently onto the blanket. The poor boy was past crying now, and was merely clutching at himself and whimpering, his eyes squeezed tightly closed.

Kyle smoothed the thick black hair back on Joey's head and murmured to him until he relaxed and stopped squinting. Still stroking Joey's hair, Kyle smiled kindly down into the boy's wide, deep, frightened blue eyes.

Kyle was frightened himself, but he knew he would never show that to the youngster. The boy needed to see strength and calmness, and he would get both from Kyle, who had learned to mask his true feelings during his years in premed.

"I'm Dr. Kyle, and this is Nurse Gracie," he said softly.

"Gracie," the boy repeated.

Kyle slid a glance in Gracie's direction. She shrugged. "We know each other."

"Good," Kyle said, knowing the boy would be more comfortable with someone he was familiar

with. Particularly if it was Gracie, who was especially good with children. "Joey, you were stung by
a wasp. Do you know what that is?"

"Bee," Joey said immediately, and once again
began clutching his arms to his chest.

"Yeah, kind of like a bee," Kyle said with a
chuckle. "A wasp sure hurts the same as a bee sting,
doesn't it, pal?"

Gracie pulled a small package of meat tenderizer
from her pack, along with a bowl and spoon. "Nathan," she said, handing the items to the older man,
"I need you to go mix up some of this with a little
bit of water. Make a paste for me."

"Yes, ma'am," Nathan agreed immediately, taking the bowl and spoon and looking relieved to have
something to do.

"Have you done any sparklers yet, Joey?" Gracie
asked the small boy as she casually ran her fingers
across his arms, his legs, his stomach and his back,
examining him for wasp stings. Her touch was so
gentle that Joey immediately calmed, warming to
the subject of fireworks, and especially sparklers.

"One here," Gracie pointed out to Kyle, gesturing to a spot just over Joey's left elbow that was
swollen from a sting. "And one here." Under Joey's
right knee. It looks a little red, but not bad.

It could have been worse. Much worse.

Kyle sent up a silent prayer of gratitude that God
had taken care of the little boy. His mind could easily imagine what *could* have happened, and he was
blessing God that it had not happened that way.

Constance hovered closely nearby, calling out encouragement to Joey and murmuring her worried thoughts to her friends. But she allowed Kyle and Gracie to do their work unhindered. It was clear the older woman put much trust in Gracie's medical abilities, Kyle realized as he watched the scene play out.

"There doesn't appear to be too much redness or swelling," Kyle commented, examining the sting sites lightly with his finger. He looked carefully at the boy's eyes and then felt his glands. "Do you have a stethoscope in that bag of yours, Gracie?"

Gracie looked genuinely affronted that he'd asked. "Of course I have a stethoscope."

Kyle wanted to shake his head in amusement. As if everyone carried stethoscopes with them as a routine matter of course.

She reached into her pack, felt around for a moment, and produced a stethoscope, which she handed to him with a flourish.

Of course.

Gracie carried a comprehensive bag of medical supplies around with her wherever she went. Just in case of an emergency.

Including, of all things, meat tenderizer to treat bee and wasp stings.

That was plain, good old common sense.

And Kyle liked it. He wished he would have thought of it.

But for now, he would take Gracie's lead in the medical arena, and thank God someone—*Gracie*—

had the presence of mind to think to bring a medical bag in the first place.

He put the stethoscope to his ears and checked the boy's heart and lungs, which sounded just fine. No signs of a possible allergic reaction.

At the same time, Gracie checked his blood pressure, nodding to let Kyle know Joey was okay as she loosened the cuff. She had her medical look on her face, the nurse's no-nonsense half smile, but Kyle could see the strain in her eyes. He thought he would be the only one to know how much the incident had frightened her.

He reached for her hand and gave it a tight squeeze, hoping she'd know what he was trying to communicate without words.

Then he turned back to his patient, who was beginning to squirm, being confined on the blanket as he was. The stings obviously weren't hurting him very much anymore, and immediate threat of an allergic reaction seemed remote, so Kyle let Joey sit up, keeping a hand on his back for support.

"We still have to put something on those sting sites, Joey, so they don't get infected. You don't want them to swell up and get sore," Gracie said, lightly dabbing a swab of alcohol on the sting wounds as Nathan returned with the bowl.

The older man knelt by the young boy and gravely held out the small bowl of paste to Gracie. His face was pinched with emotion as he wrapped his arms around the boy and brushed a soft kiss into his dark hair.

"You gave me a good scare, son," he said, his voice low and gravelly. He pulled in a ragged breath. "But you're going to be fine now. Nurse Gracie and Dr. Kyle will take good care of you."

Brushing the boy's hair out of his eyes, Nathan planted a gentle kiss on the boy's forehead, and then withdrew.

Kyle chuckled under his breath.

Meat tenderizer.

It wasn't on every doctor's medicine shelf, that was for sure, but as unconventional as it might seem to the trained eye, he had to admit it was effective for bee and wasp stings.

Gracie leveled him with a don't-say-a-word glare before smiling at Joey and stirring the bowl of paste in her hand. "Can you hold out your arm for me, sweetheart? I'm going to paint on you, okay?"

Joey's eyes were as wide as globes, but he nodded hesitantly.

"This is going to feel kind of yucky," Gracie continued, dipping the spoon in the concoction and using the back end to spread it across the wound. "But it will make those stings feel all better."

With a few dabs of meat tenderizer solution, the boy was pronounced *all better* and allowed to return to his grandmother's waiting arms, where she crooned and cooed over him. Wasp stings were already a thing of the past in Joey's young mind, and he babbled to his grandmother about sparklers and fireworks and other surprises the day's picnic was sure to bring.

"Nathan?" Constance said suddenly, turning everyone's attention to the older man. Her voice was full of alarm. "Are you okay?"

Nathan had dropped to one knee, one hand on the ground for balance. He was clutching his throat, sputtering and gasping for a breath.

Kyle, still on his knees, scrambled to Nathan's side, pulling him down to a sitting position and couching him against his own body, wrapping his arm around the man's chest for support.

Nathan was heaving for breath, and his face looked unusually red. His lips were pulled tight against his teeth, as if he were in pain.

"Nathan, buddy, did you get stung by a wasp?" Kyle asked, immediately perusing what he could see of the man's exposed skin. Kyle's gut feeling was that he had an allergic reaction going on here.

Nathan nodded roughly and yanked up his sleeve, revealing a nasty red welt swelling on his biceps. "Just this one," he rasped through a dry throat. "It's no big deal."

"I hate to differ with you," Kyle said, yanking a handkerchief from his back pocket and reaching for a sturdy straight stick he could use as leverage, "but this time, I think it's a big deal. Have you ever been stung by a wasp before?"

Nathan shrugged, then held his chest as he coughed for a breath, squeezing his eyes shut against the pain. "No. Not that I can remember."

Gracie appeared, a welcome sight to Kyle. She crouched down in front of Nathan and helped Kyle create a tourniquet from the handkerchief and stick. She seemed to know automatically what Kyle was doing, without even asking.

"You're having an allergic reaction, Nathan," she informed him crisply.

"Is that why I feel so lousy?" he joked, shrugging weakly.

"Is he going to be okay?" Constance Laughlin asked from behind Kyle's shoulder. She hovered nearby, cuddling a now sleeping Joey in her arms. "Do you think it might be serious? Do you think we need to take him to the hospital?"

Kyle wasn't sure what to do with Constance's nervous chatter, so he looked to Gracie.

Gracie was taking Nathan's blood pressure, and looked completely composed. "I don't think so, Constance," she assured calmly, in what Kyle thought of as her "nurse's voice."

To Kyle she said softly, "I have epinephrine in my bag."

Kyle was able to reach the bag without shifting too much and causing Nathan any discomfort, and he used one hand to rummage through the various items Gracie carried until he found the box containing sharps and a vial of epinephrine.

He handed them over to Gracie, who was, Kyle definitely thought, by far the expert when it came to administering shots. Gracie prepared and administered the dose of epinephrine like the professional she was, and then loosened the tourniquet and smiled at Nathan, giving him a reassuring pat on the shoulder.

"It won't be long now," she assured him. "You'll be breathing easier in just a few minutes. You should feel much better, though you won't be symptom free for a few days, yet. It wouldn't hurt to take an antihistamine, too, if you have it."

"What, you don't carry antihistamine in that pack of yours?" Kyle teased, rummaging his hand around inside her bag.

She leveled him with a scorching glare, then grinned cattily.

"I have an allergy pill," Constance said, shifting the sleeping boy in her arms so she could pull the capsule from her purse.

With a look that brooked no argument, she shoved the medicine into Nathan's hand. "Does anyone have something he can take this pill with?"

Constance sounded like a mother hen, and Kyle chuckled under his breath. Gracie caught his gaze and shared his moment of amusement.

They'd talked more than once in their many conversations about the possible inkling of romance between Constance and Nathan. This afternoon certainly appeared to confirm it.

Someone handed Nathan a cola, and he promptly popped the top and washed down the pill, giving Constance a cheeky grin as he did so. He was breathing easier now, and was sitting on his own, leaning his elbow on one knee. His color was better, too, though maybe a little flushed when he looked at Constance.

Kyle removed the tourniquet, tossed the stick away and stuffed the handkerchief back into his pocket. Gracie was busy repacking her bag, so Kyle decided to take a short walk to stretch his legs. It had been an exciting and exhausting morning, and he thought it would be good to have a moment to himself.

That solitude was not to be. Robert caught up with him moments later.

"Good work back there, pal," he said, slapping Kyle on the back and giving him a one-two punch on the arm as they had during medical school.

Kyle shook his head vehemently, waving off Robert's good-natured comments. "Gracie was the one toting the medical bag."

"Mmm," Robert agreed. "Yes, that's true. The small-town medical practitioner. That could be you, you know," he said softly.

"What's that supposed to mean?" Kyle's stomach clenched.

"Helping out here in Safe Harbor. You're needed around here. You've given this community something special of yourself, Kyle. Surely you've noticed what a difference you've made."

"I'm just filling in for you, buddy. Until your baby is born."

"No, you're not. I guess you haven't noticed, Kyle, but you haven't taken my place around here with the work you've done. You've created your own niche in this community.''

Kyle's throat went tight. Robert's words were soft and serious. And they were exactly what Kyle wanted to hear.

''What are you saying?''

Robert took him by the shoulder and looked him straight in the eye, forcing his strong, sober gaze on Kyle. ''I'm saying that I think you should stay on here, buddy. Become a partner with me at the clinic. Make Safe Harbor your *home*.''

Chapter Nine

Kyle felt as if someone had bashed him right in the gut, sucker punched the wind right out of him. He wanted to drop to his knees and gasp for air, because he couldn't breathe at all.

He tightened his lips and turned away from his friend, afraid Robert would be able to see the mixed emotions on his face.

"What is it?" Robert asked, placing a hand on Kyle's shoulder. "We've been friends a long time, Kyle. We've been through a lot of things together. You know you can talk to me."

No, he couldn't.

He couldn't talk to anyone about *this* particular problem.

He'd just been offered heaven on a platter and he couldn't even step through the pearly gates.

He hadn't been sucker punched. He'd just been stabbed through the heart.

He smiled weakly for Robert's benefit, and shrugged mildly as if it didn't matter to him. Much. "Can't say it doesn't tempt me."

"Then do it," Robert urged, making a fist and pumping it in the air. "Stay on. Make a home for yourself in Safe Harbor."

Kyle jammed his fingers through his hair. So much for pretending not to be interested. "Look, Robert, it's complicated."

His friend chuckled and shook his head. "I can't see what's complicated about it, unless you're talking about a woman. And buddy, I hate to be the one to break it to you, but when you're dealing with women, things are *always* complicated."

Kyle snorted a laugh. Robert had that right, in any case.

"The way I see it," Robert continued, "your staying on in Safe Harbor permanently is the answer to everyone's prayers."

Kyle squeezed his fists by his side. It would be the answer to *his* prayers.

But this wasn't about him.

It was about Gracie.

If he decided to stay in Safe Harbor, he'd be calling her hand. She would take it personally, and she would use it as an excuse not to leave.

She would use *him* as an excuse not to follow her dreams. And he couldn't live with that.

And even though, deep in his heart, he believed

Gracie belonged in Safe Harbor, she had to figure that out on her own, in her own time and in her own way. He would never want to be the one to tie her down so she never had the opportunity to find the truth.

Not to mention the fact that their engagement was a ruse. He couldn't very well settle down in Safe Harbor with things the way they now stood. He was engaged to a woman in the town!

What a complicated web he'd woven. Line upon line, all around himself. And now, faced with finally being offered the haven he'd always wanted, he would pay the consequences of his actions.

And he would pay with his own happiness.

"I'll think about it," he conceded to his friend, knowing Robert wouldn't easily let him off the hook. And he certainly wouldn't take no for an answer. Kyle decided he would just have to slip away unnoticed when the time was right.

"Look, I'm not saying I don't like working in Safe Harbor, because you know I do," he continued. "But I've got to pray about it. I've got to make sure I'm making the right decision."

Maybe if he would have prayed about it before he'd caught himself up in this big mess with Gracie in the first place, he wouldn't be standing here now, miserably wishing he could dig himself a big hole in the ground and cover himself up.

"I know you'll do the right thing," Robert said. "And the offer stands. I want you as my partner at the clinic, and I know Safe Harbor needs you to stay in this town. When you figure out what you're doing, you let me know, okay?''

Kyle had already figured it out. He just didn't want to face the truth.

Not today, anyway.

Gracie found herself caught up in a riotous game of volleyball with some of the older children, and when she looked up, Kyle was nowhere to be found. She asked around, thinking he might be slinging horseshoes with some of the other men or showing off more of his culinary expertise at the hot dog grill, but no one seemed to know where he'd gone.

Gracie knew he'd come to the picnic with the McGuires because she'd ridden with him, so he couldn't have gone too far away. And if he'd gone anywhere, he was hoofing it. It was likely he'd simply taken a stroll along one of the many winding paths that shot off the green and into the foothills.

She considered trying to look for him, but quickly nixed that idea. The paths snaking around the area were far too numerous for her to try them all, and she couldn't very well guess which way he'd gone, if, in fact, he'd gone for a hike at all. There were a dozen other scenarios she hadn't yet explored.

After taking one last walk around the green with an eye out for Kyle, she gave a mental shrug and decided to join Constance and Wendy and some of the other ladies of the Women's League over by the gazebo for a bit of good gossip.

She was heading in that direction when her father

appeared suddenly and cut her off at the proverbial pass.

He grasped her elbow in a firm grip and turned
her decisively back toward the tree line. His stride
was so fast she had to jog to keep up with him.

"What's wrong?" she asked, trying for lightness,
but knowing her feelings were clear on the other
side of the spectrum.

In her heart, she thought her dad might be cor-
nering her. He tended to do that when he wanted to
speak to her about something. And if she had to
spring a guess, she would guess that *something* was
none other that Dr. Kyle Hart.

Kyle was the last person Gracie wanted to talk to
her father about. She hadn't spoken to her father
about Kyle since the day they'd first announced their
engagement. Not with any depth.

Though she lived in the same house with him,
they carefully danced around the issue, making only
the most cursory of comments about her fiancé and
sidestepping any questions.

For the most part, he'd let her—and the matter of
Kyle—be. And if Gracie was allowed to have her
way, she wanted to keep it that way.

"Nothing is wrong, Gracie," answered her father
briskly, dropping his hand from her arm. "So you
can relax now. I was just wondering where that
young man of yours is right about now. Thought he
should be hanging around with you, being as you
are *engaged,* and all."

That didn't take long, Gracie thought wryly, denying her first urge to cringe. Count on her father to get right to the point.

"How should I know where Kyle is, Dad?" she snapped back, huffing out a frustrated breath. "I don't keep him on a leash."

"No need to be sarcastic with me, Gracie." Surprisingly, it wasn't his usual fatherly, condescending tone he was using, but a quiet, thoughtful expression, instead. The softness of his tone and eyes made her step back immediately.

"Sorry," she apologized hastily, feeling genuinely contrite.

It wasn't her father's fault she was upset with the way things were working out with Kyle today.

Every day.

"The truth is, I'm a little put out with *my man* right now. He didn't tell me he was leaving, and I can't find him anywhere."

They passed the line of pungent evergreens and began walking down one of the many secluded, wooded paths. Her father placed his hand back upon her elbow and continued to gently escort her along the way. This time, Gracie didn't fight him.

He chuckled at her anger. "Well, as you said, you don't keep Kyle on a leash," he reminded her, tugging at his beard with his free hand.

"Maybe, but there is such a thing as common courtesy," she snapped. "And Kyle apparently doesn't know what that means."

Her father surprised her by slapping his leg with his palm and breaking out in a full-bellied laugh.

And when she glared at him, it only made him grab for his gut and laugh even harder.

She yanked her elbow away from his grip. "What's so funny?" she demanded, planting her fists on her hips and continuing to glare at him.

He wiped his eye with his thumb, still chuckling. He made a genuine effort to stop a couple of times, but then shook his head and just kept on laughing. "You sound just like your mother."

Gracie pinched her lips and swung her hips to one side. "Great, Dad. I'm sure she'd be thrilled to hear that."

Her father's eyes widened, as if he was surprised. "She *would* be happy to hear that, Gracie. She's proud of you, you know."

Gracie snorted and shook her head in disbelief. "Oh, yeah. Right. The daughter that's made such a raving success of her life."

Now it was her father's turn to plant his beefy fists on his hips. "You sound like you don't mean what you're saying, missy."

Gracie turned away, laughing hollowly. "Oh, I believe it."

Her father turned on his heel and started walking away from her without a word. Gracie hesitated for a moment, staring at his back with her mouth practically hanging open.

A moment later, she was hurrying to catch up with him. "Daddy?"

He looked at her, his expression a mixture of pain

and disbelief. "Where have you been all these years? Are you blind, Gracie, or just dumb?"

"Ouch."

"Well, honestly. What planet are you living on? What hopeless ideal have you set for yourself? What is your impossible-to-achieve definition of what makes a person a success?"

She opened her mouth to tell him, but he held up his hands to keep her from speaking. "No, I don't want to know."

"What?"

She'd had some pretty unusual father-daughter talks with him before, but this one was a real doozy. She wasn't following at all, except that she had the strongest feeling her father was disappointed in her.

Again.

"Gracie, you have a fantastic career, one most women would be jealous of. You have the opportunity to help people every day of your life."

He paused thoughtfully. "And now you're going to get married to a rich, handsome man. Isn't that what women dream about?"

He sounded so legitimately confused Gracie wanted to sit right down in the middle of the path and cry. "Not this woman."

"Then what *are* your dreams?"

She looked away, her heart tearing in two.

This was her father. He had never listened to her before. Why now?

"Tell me," he urged, taking a step closer to her but not making physical contact. "I can feel something is wrong with you lately, Gracie. I see it every time I sit with you at the breakfast table. And if there's something I can do to make things right, I aim to do that for my only daughter. Is it Kyle?''

''Dad,'' she said, her voice cracking, ''my dreams haven't changed since high school.''

''Meaning?''

Did she have to spell it out for him? She wanted to scream at him for not knowing.

He *should* know. He was the one who kept her from them in the first place.

''I want to be a missionary, like you and Mom. Travel and see the world. Go somewhere where I can really *help* people in need, not be trapped in this tiny town forever.''

Douglass stopped walking and moved to the side of the path, carefully seating himself on a large rock. He looked at her for a long while without speaking. His gaze was kind and thoughtful, and Gracie was afraid to move or speak herself.

He opened his mouth once or twice as if he were going to say something, but then clamped his jaw closed again as if thinking better of it.

Gracie couldn't think of anything witty to say, and she was terrified of what her father would say when he finally got around to speaking. She'd never been this open with him before. She'd always been one to speak her mind—except with her daddy.

But she was a little angry with him, too.

He was the one who'd made the decision to leave her behind when her parents had become missionaries to Ecuador. He was the one who'd determined it was better for her to become educated in the States, even when she'd tearfully begged and pleaded with her whole soul to let her come with them.

He was the one who had shattered her dreams when she was only fifteen years old.

"Gracie."

She looked at her father.

"Where were you just now?" he queried softly. "You didn't answer when I talked to you. Not even when I said your name."

She frowned.

"I have a couple of things I want to say to you, and I don't know that you're ready to hear them at this present moment. But I'm going to go ahead and say them anyway, because you need to hear them, and because I need to say them."

She didn't speak. Couldn't speak. She was so choked up it was a wonder she could breathe. Though she mentally and emotionally geared up all her defenses, knowing whatever was coming would most likely knock her off her feet.

"Gracie, when you were fifteen you wanted to go with us to Ecuador on our mission. You imagined some kind of glamorous missionary lifestyle, I think, where you'd be flitting around some little Amazon jungle tribe's village handing each of the natives a Bible in their own language. And where everyone would immediately see and love the Jesus you know in your heart.

"Maybe you still think it's that way, I don't know," he said, cocking his head at her. "I still see that gleam in your eyes."

"I'm not a child anymore," she protested, her voice raspy.

"No, you're not," he agreed with a nod. He tugged thoughtfully on his beard. "And I hope, now that you're an *adult,* that you can see, in hindsight, the reasons we had for leaving you State-side."

Gracie's heart froze in her chest. She would never understand a father's reason for leaving his daughter at home while he went gallivanting off to another country. There were not enough words in the world.

Douglass could clearly see his daughter's reaction, for his smile was patient, and a little pained. "You don't know how hard it was to leave you behind, do you, Gracie? Do you think your mother and I got on the plane and forgot we had a daughter?"

Gracie shrugged.

"Be realistic. We weren't thinking about ourselves at all, Gracie. We were thinking of you." He tussled his hair, making it stand on end. "What we did was what was best for you at the time. You got an excellent education here, Gracie, something you might not have had as a missionary's kid."

Gracie wrapped her arms around herself. What scared her the most was that he was beginning to make a weird kind of sense.

"Because you remained in the United States, Gracie, you had the opportunity for higher education. You became a certified nurse.'' He gave her a pointed look. ''*Now* you can go wherever you want in the world with the education and training necessary to really make a difference in people's lives.''

''What?'' She choked on the word.

''You heard me.''

''What do you mean, I can go wherever I want in the world? I have obligations here in Safe Harbor, thanks to you leaving me here to find my own life. I can't just *leave*.''

Her father shook his head and then gave his white beard a good tug. He stared her down for a good moment before speaking. ''Gracie, the only thing keeping you in Safe Harbor is you.''

Gracie blanched. ''If that nonsense is supposed to be some weird kind of cockeyed fatherly philosophy, it isn't funny.''

''It isn't philosophy, Gracie. It's truth. And I think you'll be able to see it for yourself, when you sit down and think about it.'' He raised one brow, challenging her to heed his words.

She wanted to cover her ears with the palms of her hands and run away screaming, like she used to do when she was a toddler and didn't like what she heard her father saying to her. But not only was it juvenile, she knew it wouldn't do any good.

She'd already heard the worst.

Her father was placing the blame on *her* for her own failure.

''That being said,'' her father continued, as if he had not or could not see her obvious distress, ''I really think you ought to consider staying on in Safe Harbor.''

Gracie made a choking noise, but her father didn't appear to hear it.

''You've really made a difference here. You're looking into the big, wide world to find meaning, when you've *made* meaning for yourself right here. You're looking so far ahead that you're missing the obvious.

''You're right in saying people need you around here. They do. You're part of the fabric, the weave of Safe Harbor. You won't find that in Ecuador, or anywhere else in the world. One thing your mother and I have learned—there's only one place you can call home. And Safe Harbor? Well, there's no place like it.''

''I don't want to talk about this,'' she said, her head swimming. First he said one thing, then he said the opposite. And that's what she was feeling—as if she were being pulled in polar opposites.

She wasn't sure how to feel about what her father was telling her. She didn't want to feel anything at all.

Her life was already too complicated with her *engagement* to Kyle. With the web of lies and deceit she'd inadvertently formed.

Now this.

''You're a bit too old for me to be giving you lectures,'' her father continued, as if he hadn't heard her desire to end this painful conversation, ''but if I were you, why, I'd—''

Gracie lit out along the first side path they drew upon, running as fast and as far as her feet would carry her.

Away from her father.

She was vaguely aware that she was running uphill, away from the crowded green at Safe Harbor and the safety of other people, but it was only by the way that her muscles burned as her legs pumped and how her lungs heaved with every breath that she could even tell which direction she was running.

Far away was good. Another planet would be even better.

The pink, dusky look in the sky was a warning she ought not travel too far all alone in the growing darkness, but right now she needed to run, to put some distance between her and—

Thud.

She'd turned a sharp corner in the path without slowing her pace, and had run headlong into—what? A tree? A rock? Something that had all the give of a brick wall.

Except for that something groaned when he was hit, and snaked his arms around her so she wouldn't fall from the impact.

Kyle.

"Gracie!" he said, equally surprised. He kept his arms securely around her waist and gently pulled her to the forest floor next to him, tucking her into the crook of his arm.

She heaved for breath, the wind completely knocked out of her and her head swirling with surprise. Still, she didn't miss the feeling of *rightness* at being once more within the circle of Kyle's arms.

"Gracie, this is the middle of the wilderness," he said next to her ear. "What in the world are you doing out here alone?"

"Not looking for you," she snapped, glaring at him for good measure.

It occurred to her to point out the obvious, that he was her supposed *fiancé* and that if she shouldn't be out here *alone,* it was *his fault.* He, after all, had been the one to leave her alone in the first place.

Kyle looked at her as if she'd lost her mind. "No, of course you weren't looking for me. I mean—I didn't tell you where I was going, did I?"

There was a pregnant pause, where Gracie's gaze stated the obvious.

At least he had the common courtesy to appear chagrined.

"No, you did not tell me where you were going, thank you very much."

He chuckled, then kissed her on the cheek. "Thank you for worrying about me."

"I was not—" Gracie started, sitting up and looking at him. Then she stopped herself. There were already enough lies told in this summer. "Oh, Kyle!"

"What were you doing, Gracie? You're completely out of breath. I thought I knew you pretty well, but I've never known you to be a jogger, especially not on a holiday."

She gave him her best pout. "I was running away from my father, if you must know."

She decided on honesty, knowing Kyle would extract the truth from her eventually anyway. Somehow, she couldn't keep the truth from him. Besides, she'd already had enough lies to last a lifetime.

Kyle rolled to his feet and offered his hand to her to help her stand up. "Have you caught your breath enough to start walking back toward the green? It's beginning to get dark, and we don't want to get caught in the woods overnight."

He winked, making her heart turn over.

She nodded and a took few sips from the canteen of cool water he offered her. He, at least, had *planned* his hike to some degree. He had water and a pocketknife strapped to his belt.

She, on the other hand, had nothing.

"So what did your father say to you?" Kyle asked curiously when they had been walking in silence for a minute. "Whatever it was that sent you screaming and running, I mean?"

"I wasn't screaming," she denied hotly, scorching him with a glare.

Kyle nodded, a smile tugging at his mouth. "Oh. Right. No screaming."

"He said, and I quote, 'Gracie, the only thing keeping you in Safe Harbor is you.'" She nearly choked on the words, having to say them to Kyle.

Kyle stopped walking and turned toward her. The smile was gone from his eyes and his jaw was tight. "And what do you think?"

''What do *you* think?''

He shook his head. ''I'm not the one that matters here. But if you're asking, I think your father's dead-on right on this one, Gracie.''

She stared at him in disbelief. He was taking her father's side.

''You have had it in your heart to achieve your dreams all this time. You only had to figure it out for yourself.''

''Oh, terrific. And you're only now telling me this, why?''

Kyle laughed harshly. ''What good would it have done for me to say something?''

She shook her head in hot denial.

''What good is it doing me to talk about it now? You still aren't ready to hear it.'' He pinned her with his gaze, daring her to deny what he'd said.

Gracie spun away from him and started marching down the mountain, leaving Kyle in her tracks. She was angry, the steam-pouring-out-the-ears kind of angry, but not at Kyle.

Not even at her father.

At herself.

Because she'd had a revelation back on the trail that she couldn't deny. The men in her life were only looking out after her best interests. They were telling her the truth because they wanted her to succeed.

And she knew they were right.

She'd been using Safe Harbor as an excuse to hide for years.

Chapter Ten

"Gracie, wait up." Kyle jogged to catch up to her, the dirt flying up at his heels. "Come on. Don't run off on me."

"I'm not running," she said with a dry laugh, clutching at her side to catch her breath. She met his gaze as he approached. "I don't think I have it in me to run anymore."

"Literally or figuratively?"

"Both. I definitely shouldn't have run up that hill away from my father," she said, grimacing in pain. "I can barely move my legs anymore. And my back is absolutely killing me."

"And your heart?" he queried in a rich, soft voice that gave Gracie warm shivers. His gaze was as warm as his voice.

She lifted two fingers to her neck and pretended to feel for a pulse, acting as if she couldn't find it

for a moment, and then suddenly smiling and nodding. "Still beating."

Kyle grinned at her antics, but didn't let her off
the hook with his question. "That's not what I
meant, and you know it."

Gracie shook her head and reached for Kyle's
hand, linking her fingers with his. His hand was big
and strong and warm, and the squeeze he gave her
fingers was familiar and comforting. She felt as if
she could hold his hand forever. "Give me some
time to work through this, okay?"

"Haven't I been doing just that?" He pulled her
closer to him.

"Why are you being so nice to me?" It occurred
to her that she didn't deserve his friendship, never
mind the support he was giving her now. She'd
made all the mistakes, and he'd stuck by her side
through absolutely everything.

He grinned widely and raised his eyebrows. "Because I like you."

He held up his hand when she would have protested. "No, Gracie, I won't hear it, so just save
your voice for bigger and better things."

He turned to her, squeezing her hand to let her
know how much he meant his words. "If you accept
one thing today, it's going to be that I *want* to be
here with you right now."

"I can see that you're serious," she conceded reluctantly, her heart soaring as his words soothed her
fears. "But what I can't figure out for the life of me
is *why?*"

They reached the edge of the tree line where they could see the crowd of people on the green, but Kyle pulled her back into the trees where they would still be hidden. "Fourth of July, fireworks, a pretty lady. What's there to understand?"

Gracie had to laugh at his blithe reply. It reaffirmed hope, though her confusion remained. "Then is it all right for me to appreciate the undeniably charming company of a handsome man for this Independence Day celebration?"

"Well, it's evening," Kyle pointed out, gesturing to the green and the town full of happy people, enjoying each other's company and the provisions of the picnic, "but you're welcome to my company."

Gracie looked out to see her friends and neighbors milling around, preparing for the fireworks display to come. Most had brought blankets and were spread out under the dusky evening sky, chatting with each other, tossing footballs and baseballs, and waving sparklers in the already darkening night sky. Dogs ran barking across the green and little boys wrestled on the lawn.

Gracie smiled, remembering how much she'd enjoyed waving sparklers when she was a girl. Now there were enough fireworks in her life without lighting a match to anything, thank you very much.

"I don't think I'm quite ready to go back down there, Kyle" she said softly, pulling her hand from Kyle's and wrapping her arms around herself. It suddenly felt chilly, though the evening was warm.

"Then don't." Kyle's voice was unusually

coarse, and Gracie's gaze flew to his. He was smiling, an almost secretive expression on his face and a light glow in his amber eyes.

"We can't stay up here all night." Much as she'd like to stay, perhaps forever.

He held up both hands, palm out, waving them like a stop sign. "I will be right back, Gracie. Don't move a muscle."

She watched as he darted back into the trees and disappeared from view. He was gone a long time—so long that Gracie thought seriously about returning to the green alone, to where the McGuires were picnicking, to wait for him. He'd have to return there eventually.

Suddenly he appeared behind her, startling her with his voice over her shoulder. She hadn't seen or heard him coming. "Over here, Gracie."

She put a hand to her chest to still her racing heart, and reached out her other hand for his arm. "Where did you come from?"

"Over there," he said, pointing to a grove of pine trees. "I was—*retrieving* a few items."

In his other hand, he carried the picnic basket she remembered seeing earlier in the McGuires' Suburban. The one with the snakes. She smiled, hoping there were no more of *those* sorts of surprises within the pretty wicker basket.

Kyle set the basket on the ground and searched within it until he pulled out an old-fashioned, red-checkered blanket, which he then laid out on the ground with a flourish.

Here, in this little spot of green, they would be invisible to the Safe Harbor crowd, but would have a good view of the fireworks to come.

"I'll bet we'll be able to see the fireworks from here just fine," he commented, gesturing for her to take a seat on the blanket. He seated himself next to her, rustling once again within the basket for more goodies he could present to her.

Within minutes, he had laid out a feast for her—rolled, thinly sliced meat; chunks of cheddar, Muenster, and mozzarella cheese; a variety of fruits and melons, and even fresh-baked fudge brownies.

She knew without asking that he'd prepared everything himself. She remembered the night at her house when he'd cooked a full gourmet meal for her.

Again today, he'd surprised her with his thoughtfulness and talent. He really was an extraordinary man.

She picked up a wedge of soft Muenster cheese and nibbled at the corner. "You had this little picnic for two planned all along, didn't you?"

It wasn't an accusation so much as a realization. He hadn't come here unprepared.

He shrugged and popped a beef roll into his mouth, chewing slowly and swallowing before he answered. "Not exactly in this way. How could I possibly have known? But I'll admit I was hoping we'd have some time alone together."

"That was very thoughtful," she said softly, curling an arm around her knee.

"I was thinking of you," he admitted, his voice low and rough.

She looked up, and her gaze met his. His eyes were warm with affection. She swallowed hard. "Have I been a complete idiot?"

He shook his head, his eyes gleaming. A smile played at his mouth, but didn't stay, as his gaze grew dark. "No more than I."

She waited for him to explain, not even daring to breathe.

"I had a few revelations of my own today. Things that should have been obvious, but weren't. Things I need to think long and hard about." He broke his gaze away from her so she couldn't read his expression.

"Like what?" He spoke as if he were talking about her problems, yet clearly he was speaking about himself. It was the oddest sensation.

Had something bad happened that had sent him off alone, hiking in the woods? Had he been running away, in a sense, just as she had?

He stretched out on the blanket, propping his chin in his hand and just looking at her for a minute, a half smile on his face.

"Things," he said evasively.

She rolled to her stomach and slanted in close to him, propping her chin on her palms and leaning in just until her breath mingled with his. She paused, just over his lips. "So," she said slowly, smiling because she knew she had the upper hand. "What is Dr. Kyle Hart running from? I really want to know.''

''That's not important.'' His brows were low and his voice was gruff.

She reached up and stroked a slow line from his firm, clean-shaven jaw to his square chin, reveling in the strength she found there. ''It is to me.''

He chuckled, but instead of answering her, he kissed her.

It wasn't the answer she wanted, but she wasn't in any position to complain. As he reached up to cradle her head in his hand, brushing the hair gently away from her face and raining soft kisses upon her, fireworks started shooting off above them, showering the night sky with patriotic red, white and blue.

Her father's words washed over her as the fireworks lit up the night sky.

The only one keeping you back is you.

She was free. She could go. Wherever she wanted in the world, the doors were open to her.

Kyle was communicating as much in his fervent kiss, in the strength and gentleness of his touch. He *believed* in her, and in what she could accomplish in the world when she was ready to do so.

She was free to go.

So why did she suddenly feel so much like staying?

Even two weeks after the Fourth of July outing with Gracie, Kyle was so bewildered he didn't know whether he was coming or going.

Actually, that wasn't quite true. He was perfectly aware that he was *going*.

He just didn't want to be.

The more time he spent with Gracie, the more he realized how much he needed her in his life.

How much more time he wanted to be able to spend with her.

A lifetime, perhaps.

Granted, he and Gracie didn't do many of the things he'd typically consider young couples did. They didn't see movies together, and they rarely ate out. Certainly never as a date.

But they did do their grocery shopping together, attend the First Peninsula Church together every Sunday morning and they took food and medicine to those who lived in the dock district.

He had even let Gracie trim his hair once, though he'd made her promise to take off no more than the split ends. He still wasn't positive he trusted the woman with sharp objects, he thought with a grin.

These things they did—these were the sorts of activities *married* people pursued. And he'd slipped into that role with relative ease.

There were times he poked tentatively at his past, but he found the memories didn't come back to haunt him so readily anymore. They were more like precious keepsakes, to be taken out and treasured, and then carefully replaced to take out another time.

He wouldn't trade the time he had with Melody for the world. His time with Melody had been good, and right. But he had finally realized he was ready to move on with his life.

Only, he had made that realization a little too late. It didn't matter how he felt now, or what decisions he'd made about his life.

Gracie was headed out of Safe Harbor, and so, by necessity, was he.

If only Gracie would see, as he had, what a great team they made when they were together. They naturally complemented one another, as if they had been made for one another.

He thought perhaps, though he knew Gracie would never consider to see it this way, that they *had* been made for one another.

Take today, for example.

He was in Gracie's small but efficient little blue Focus, on his way to pick up Mrs. Baske for a re-check on her blood pressure. For some reason, the old woman had taken to him, and allowed him to bully her into coming in to the clinic, as long as he, personally, picked her up for the ride.

Gracie supported his efforts, insisting that she would just be in the way if she accompanied him down to pick Mrs. Baske up.

He didn't agree, but she insisted.

He pulled up in front of Mrs. Baske's small, run-down clapboard house, if it could even be classified as a house, and decided he'd look into getting some paint for the place. Surely it couldn't take more than a day for him and Gracie to plaster a new coat of paint onto the old wood, and maybe it would help keep drafts down a little bit.

He didn't know how Mrs. Baske could stand it, but she was so strong and resilient, Kyle didn't imagine anything could get her down.

He suspected she'd seen a lot of pain in her lifetime. She spoke often of losing her husband of forty-seven years, quite suddenly of a heart attack several years back. Gracie and Kyle had enjoyed her many stories, and Kyle wished he could do more for her than just bring her bits of food now and then.

Mrs. Baske was just one of the many reasons Kyle wanted to stay in Safe Harbor.

Permanently.

He knocked on Mrs. Baske's door, and was immediately ushered in by her usual cheerful greeting. She couldn't get around very well, but that didn't stop her from greeting her guests with vigor from the comfort of her armchair.

"Are you ready to go?" he asked as she reached over to the side table and tucked her purse under her arm. He took her elbow and helped her to stand, then guided her slowly to the door.

"You don't have to baby me, Kyle," she scolded cheerfully. "I can walk on my own. Not very fast, mind you, but you know the old story about the tortoise and the hare, don't you?"

"Sure, I know that one," he replied, winking flirtatiously at her. "I just don't get the opportunity to escort beautiful women around very often. Humor me, will you please?"

She chuckled and clucked her tongue at him. "You are a rascal, aren't you?"

He shrugged and grinned cheekily. "I guess I do what I can."

"Yes, I guess you do," she replied wryly, giving him a good stare that told him she knew exactly what he was about. "And as for escorting beautiful women, you're lying through your teeth, young man."

He always got a kick out of her calling him a *young man,* and he laughed loudly and put his arm around the old woman.

"You've been escorting a beautiful woman all over town this summer," Mrs. Baske said, patting Kyle's arm in affirmation. "Gracie Adams is the most beautiful woman in Safe Harbor."

"Yes, ma'am, she is." Kyle was in total agreement on that point. If someone were to ask him, he'd probably have to say Gracie was the most beautiful woman on the continent, maybe even in the world. But he knew he was partial, and probably getting carried away by his feelings for her.

He situated Mrs. Baske comfortably in the car and they started the short trip to the clinic before Mrs. Baske spoke again.

"It must be fantastic to be engaged to such a wonderful woman," she commented mildly, sliding him a shadowed glance that let Kyle know she meant more than she was saying aloud. "You must feel truly blessed to be with Gracie."

He opened his mouth to answer, to tell her how

blessed he was to be with Gracie. How wonderful this summer had been for him.

That, at least, would be the truth. But it was couched in a lie, and suddenly he knew he couldn't lie anymore.

"Mrs. Baske, I haven't been completely honest with you," he admitted, his voice low and coarse as he admitted his wrongdoing. "I am not...that is, Gracie and I are not..."

"Engaged," Mrs. Baske cheerfully supplied for him. "I know."

"You know?" His voice was suddenly high and squeaky as his throat closed around his breath. "But how? How long?"

She chuckled merrily, her gray eyes shining. "Since the beginning, Kyle. And don't let that surprise you."

He shook his head in disbelief.

She smiled. "I've known Gracie all her life. I know when she's trying to pull one over on me. She's never been a good liar, and in this case, she was squirming all over the place."

She chuckled, then coughed and held her chest. "I may be old, Kyle, but I'm not blind. *Yet.*" She coughed again, then laughed at herself.

"Don't hold it against Gracie," Kyle pleaded, his voice earnest. "I know it's hard to understand, but she has her reasons for wanting—*needing*—this charade. She's a good woman."

"You don't have to convince me. And I think I

can guess at her reasons. But right now, it's not
Gracie I'm thinking about.''

"No?" Kyle pulled into the clinic parking lot and
parked the car, shutting off the engine and turning
his attention to the old woman.

"No." She stared at him.

"Mrs. Baske, if you are going to blame anyone
for this charade, blame me. I am the one at fault.''

Her eyes gleamed. "That's a very noble gesture,
Kyle. And it makes me more certain than ever that
I want to do this.''

"Do what?" he queried curiously, laying his arm
across the top of the seat.

"I have something I want to give you before we
go in, Kyle.'' She pulled her purse onto her lap, then
rummaged through it for a moment.

Suddenly she pulled her hand out and smiled in
satisfaction. "Here we go."

She reached out her closed fist, holding it shakily
before him. When she lifted her eyebrows, he held
out his hand, hardly daring to breathe.

She placed something small and hard in his palm,
closing his fingers around it and giving his hand a
tight squeeze. She held his fist that way a moment,
her eyes closed and a smile on her face.

"This was my grandmother's," she said so softly
he could barely hear the words.

"I— But I—" he protested over a lump of emotion that had welled in his throat. He didn't understand, but he knew this was a big moment.

"Kyle, don't argue with an old woman. You'll

never win, and it's bad manners. Besides, you haven't even looked at it yet.''

He didn't have to look at whatever was in his palm to know it was something truly special, something really meaningful. He could see that fact on Mrs. Baske's face. But he slowly uncurled his hand nonetheless, his breath coming in short gasps.

"Oh, no. Mrs. Baske, I can't!'' he protested right away when he saw the antique diamond ring in his palm.

It was a silver ring, with eight small diamonds carefully set in a diamond shape around a much larger stone. All shone with brilliance, and Kyle knew they were the real thing.

"Mrs. Baske, the sentimental value alone makes it worth—''

"Precisely. That is why I want you to have it,'' she explained patiently, as if to a child. "I don't have a son or daughter to pass my heritage on to, but if I *did* have a son, I'd want him to be just like you. Honest and strong and charming and gallant— and most definitely as handsome as King David in the Bible.''

Kyle made a choking sound out of the back of his throat, and gripped the bottom of the steering wheel to reign in his emotions.

He wanted to tell Mrs. Baske she had picked the wrong person. He wasn't any of those things. He wasn't strong or gallant. And he'd proved today that he certainly wasn't honest.

Yet somehow Mrs. Baske's faith in him gave him

faith in himself. He looked inward and upward, and found something he didn't have before.

"You and Gracie see people's needs in the community, and you *do* something about them. You don't turn your back on what's hurting in the world. You've got a good heart, Dr. Kyle, and don't you let anyone tell you differently."

Kyle held the ring up, turning it in his fingers and letting it catch the light. "But Mrs. Baske, I just told you, Gracie and I—"

She cut in. "You want to stay in Safe Harbor, don't you?"

His gaze flew to hers. She looked amused, and strangely wise.

He nodded.

She nodded also, as if it were a given. "Well, then, you need a ring."

"I need a ring," he repeated dumbly, still staring at the glittering item.

"I need a ring," he said with more force as the idea took hold.

She chuckled, nodding again. This was where she meant to go. "Exactly."

He stared at the shiny ring, and then stared at Mrs. Baske.

It wasn't a *bad* idea.

He hadn't actually seriously considered doing a one-eighty. What if he stood up and fought for what he wanted? What if he did what he thought would be the best for both of them, instead of sitting back and letting life pass him right by?

Because of his feelings for her, he was bowing to Gracie's wishes. But in doing so, he realized suddenly, he was ruining any chance either one of them had for a happy future.

Or at least, a happy future *together*.

But what if he could convince her to stay?

What if he could convince her that happiness was possible right here in her own backyard? What if he could convince her she was making a difference here and now, in his life and in the lives of many others around her in Safe Harbor?

Hope sprang up like a wellspring within his heart. Happy endings raced through his mind.

Was it possible?

Did his bleak future stand a chance of being torched with a beacon of light as bright as the Safe Harbor lighthouse itself?

There was one way to find out.

Chapter Eleven

Tuesday afternoon, Gracie made her way to the Safe Harbor Women's League meeting with more than a little bit of trepidation in her heart.

She was about to tell them of her future plans—more or less—and seek their prayers and guidance on the matters facing her.

These were the women who'd supported her virtually all her life. She knew they would support her now when she was getting ready to leave.

If that was what she was doing.

She wasn't so sure anymore. Her heart and mind were so confused, she didn't know what she wanted.

Or rather, she was too stubborn to admit to anyone but herself that the lofty goals and dreams she'd always aspired to no longer held the siren song they once had for her. She no longer often dreamed of distant soil and foreign people.

Something new had taken their place.

Someone new.

If she could somehow disentangle herself from the tangled web she had woven around herself and Kyle, she might just try to convince a certain handsome doctor to stick around for a while, to make Safe Harbor his permanent home.

But that was neither here nor there, for Kyle was leaving, and so was she, just as soon as Wendy's baby was born and Dr. McGuire no longer needed the extra support Kyle offered. He would be out of a job, and she would be out of a fiancé.

She had already filed preliminary forms with her missionary agency of choice, a nondenominational agency out of Green Bay. She'd filled out her application on July fifth, before she put it off again and lost her nerve. Talking to Kyle and her father had motivated her to action, even if it was in a sense of desperation.

And things were looking good in that department. Not surprisingly, they needed as many nurses as they could get to join their teams. She knew that with the generous contributions First Peninsula would give, and contacts she had with a few other churches who aided her parents, not to mention her own savings, her support would be raised within a short time frame.

Kenya, she was on her way. The country she'd dreamed of visiting since she was a child.

So where was the excitement she expected to feel standing at the tip of her exhilarating future? All she was feeling now was a big, heavy lump in her stomach that made her a little woozy.

She brushed the feelings off and strode into the lighthouse meeting room, determined to make a good show no matter how she was feeling. All of her dear friends were here, talking, gossiping and in general making merry.

Gracie remembered times when she internally rolled her eyes at such small-town behavior, though not at the women themselves; yet now, it felt endearing. Comfortable. As if she were experiencing a little piece of home sweet home.

She would miss her dear friends, and she knew a moment of panic wondering if she would ever be able to make friends like these, friends who really understood her in her happy moods and her sad.

After all, some of these women had seen her toddle around in diapers, and had watched her pitch her first winning game of softball. They knew her moods because they knew *her,* inside and out. Safe Harbor was the only place she would find that level of understanding.

But wasn't that exactly what she was trying to get away from?

She didn't know anymore.

She took a plate of fresh carrot cake and sat down next to Wendy, chatting with her about her pregnancy, which was just about at term. Wendy was more than anxious to have the baby born soon, what with an active kindergartner and a wiggly preschooler already at home.

"Maybe I should try jumping jacks or something, huh, Gracie?" Wendy teased. "I'd do just about anything at this point."

Gracie laughed and shook her head. "No jumping jacks. You should walk, Wendy. Get out in the fresh air and stretch yourself out. It'll make you feel better and ease things along a bit."

"Anyone up for a twenty-mile stroll?" Wendy called out, and everyone laughed. "No, really. I'm serious. I want to have this baby."

It was a few more minutes before Constance Laughlin pulled Gracie aside, taking Gracie's cake and setting it on a nearby table before pulling her away from the general crowd.

"I can't help but notice you're not quite yourself today, sweetheart," she said, soothing a hand down Gracie's arm.

That was the understatement of the year.

And it was exactly what Gracie had been thinking about, the small-town kind of concern that would notice such details about her. A friend that would notice she was having difficulties.

It made her wince inside.

"I'm okay," she said softly. "I just have a lot on my mind."

"Well, honey, I've been there, done that. *Recently.*" She chuckled. "And it was you, Gracie, who helped me out the most, you know, in working out my problems. Not that I still don't encounter moments of confusion. But what you said to me at

Wendy's shower made sense to me, and that's what I've tried to do.''

Gracie shook her head. ''I wish you wouldn't listen to me, Constance. I don't have a clue what I'm talking about.''

''Oh, yes, you do. Your words were far wiser than your age, straight from a heart open to the Lord.''

She hugged Gracie around the shoulders. ''I recognize good advice when I hear it. And now I'm going to do you a favor and give your words back to you.''

Gracie really, *really* didn't want to hear her own words quoted back to her right now. It was so easy to be *wise* when it wasn't your own life you were talking about. Maybe she would learn to keep her big mouth shut from now on.

Constance didn't seem to notice her discomfort, or her pinched expression. She continued as if nothing were wrong.

''Now, I probably don't remember this word for word, but I recall that you reminded me that God is in charge of everything. He's got it covered, you know? And that even though it might seem really confusing to you and me, He's got it all going around the way He wants. He is in control. And in the end, what really matters is what's in your heart.''

''That does sound rather philosophical, doesn't it?'' Gracie asked wryly. ''And it sounds like something I'd say when I didn't know better.''

''It sounds like plain, good sense,'' Constance replied briskly, tapping Gracie on the shoulder with an empty paper plate for emphasis. "And one can never have enough good sense. Seek the Lord, dear, and follow your heart."

"But I haven't even told you what's bothering me," Gracie pointed out. It seemed like a fairly big omission to her.

Constance laughed and shook her head. "You don't need to tell me. I don't even need to know. This is a win-win formula. A never-fail solution. God never, ever goes wrong."

Except that Gracie *had* been seeking God, praying fervently for answers to her dilemma.

The problem wasn't that she wasn't seeking God. The problem was she wasn't finding Him.

She had even sought out the advice of Justine, a minister at First Peninsula and a good friend. She hadn't poured out her whole story, but she'd said enough to hear Justine reassure her that God, indeed, was there through all her trouble.

Deep down, Gracie knew in her heart that God wasn't the One who moved. She was the one who'd lied her way through the summer. But she was still trying to find her bearings, and it was rough terrain.

"I would like to tell everyone a little about what's going on in my life," she said, determined to move forward, knowing she needed prayer if she was going to get anywhere. Wherever God wanted her.

The tricky part, she knew, was that she could not yet blow her cover, for Kyle's sake if not for her own. She didn't want Kyle to lose his job prematurely—not until it was supposed to happen.

And she wasn't quite ready to leave.

It was not yet time to officially break things off with Kyle—not until after Wendy's baby made his or her appearance.

So she couldn't very well tell the women—her friends—that she was running off to the mission field. Yet she felt compelled to tell them something.

She needed their support now more than ever. She knew they would be her prayer warriors when she was out on the fields in Kenya, and she knew they'd pray her through the anguish she was experiencing now. If only she could express what she needed without giving herself away as a fraud.

Constance called the women into a group and announced that Gracie wanted to share something with them. Gracie was quivering inside as she pulled up a chair and looked each of her longtime friends in the eye. Their gazes were mildly curious and full of kindness and caring. Gracie found herself relaxing and opening up within the circle of their love and acceptance.

"As you know, this has been a particularly busy summer for me," she began, coughing and gasping when her voice didn't quite work properly. "Quite a lot has happened to me."

"You must mean a certain handsome doctor, if I'm not mistaken," said Wendy, running a hand over her abdomen and giving Gracie a sly wink. "I know how irresistible those doctors are. I married one."

Kyle, *irresistible?*

Gracie sighed inwardly. She might as well admit it. That was about it in a nutshell. And it had little to do with him being a doctor.

"Kyle is part of it, I guess," she admitted reluctantly to the curious group. Heat rushed to her face, and she put one hand to her cheek. Some of the ladies chuckled.

"The thing is, as much as my life has changed this summer, that is at least as much again as it's going to change once the summer is over. Things are really going to start moving."

She heard murmurs of agreement.

And approval.

Gracie tensed. They still all thought she was talking about Kyle. It was breaking her up inside not to just blurt out the truth. She ached to tell them what a mess she'd made of everything. But she stoically pulled herself together, sticking with her original plan.

"My whole life is going to change," she said, trying again to express her heart without giving herself away. "Change is imminent. Nothing is going to be the same at all."

"Getting married is a big step in anyone's life, Gracie," said the elderly Elizabeth Neal, who had lost her own sweetheart in the Korean War and had never married herself. "But you need to look at all the changes flying at you as positive things in your life, something that will improve your life and bring you much joy as you move forward."

Gracie thought of the mission field. Kenya. She'd

dreamed of being a missionary since she was a child. She'd aspired to heal people's bodies with medicine and their hearts with the love of God. To walk among those who needed her and make a real difference in their lives, to really count for something.

Now, it was all becoming a reality, thanks to Dr. Kyle Hart.

These *were* positive changes. They *would* bring her much joy.

Wouldn't they?

"But how can you be sure?" she asked, leaning forward, her elbows on her knees, eager to hear whatever answer the ladies could offer.

"Life offers no guarantees." This quiet, ragged bit of wisdom was from Constance. She of all people knew the depth of heartache life could throw a person. Yet she was still here, having grown stronger for the trials she'd encountered.

Would that be how it was with Gracie?

Would she become a stronger person because of what she'd been through this summer? She was already a better person because of having known Kyle.

The ladies misread the emotions that must have crossed her face. They stood and clamored all over her, everyone talking at once. Gracie was in a confused muddle, listening to everyone.

"Have you set a date yet, dear?"

"We want to throw a shower for you."

"Did you pick a china pattern?"

"Have you begun your premarital counseling with Pastor Burns yet?"

The questions were too much, and Gracie rose to her feet. She felt as if she was strangling, as if the world was closing in around her in a big whoosh of air. Her head was spinning dizzily.

"I'm sorry. I can't do this."

Not a moment longer.

She couldn't stand there and lie to her dear friends. And she couldn't tell them the truth. So she would do the only other thing she could think of to do.

She would leave.

And not just leave the Women's League meeting.

Leave Safe Harbor.

For good.

Chapter Twelve

Kyle was walking, but to nowhere in particular. His hands buried deep in the front pockets of his jeans, he wandered up and down around Market Square. He'd been there for hours, staring vacantly into the same windowed storefronts, kicking rocks off the sidewalk with his scuffed black cowboy boots, and staring blankly off into space.

Gracie was gone.

She'd been gone for over a week. And she'd left without a word to him. She'd taken leave at the hospital and made sure her shifts were well covered, and had even left instructions with her mother and father, of all people, on delivering some anonymous gifts to the dock district on Saturdays, knowing the people there would understand the affection behind the gift, and know without asking that the *anonymous donor* had not forgotten them.

But she had forgotten him.

Kyle wanted to kick himself.

He'd waited too long to tell her how he really felt, and now it was too late.

He should have said something that very first day, he realized now, when he had the ring Mrs. Baske had given him.

Earlier than that, even, if he would have had the guts to face up to his own feelings.

But he'd waited.

Now she'd run off to Africa without even having the courtesy to say goodbye.

She *owed* him that much. And she was a strong enough woman to own up to her obligations.

Yet to the bare eye, it looked like she was running away. At least it did to him.

And she'd left him holding the bag. What was he supposed to tell their friends and neighbors about their relationship? Did she expect him to keep up the ruse, or was he supposed to end the charade?

One person who didn't need the truth was Gracie's father. Kyle had decided to come clean with Douglass as soon as he'd realized Gracie was gone, but Gracie's father had surprised him by announcing that he and her mother already knew they weren't engaged, and had known since the very beginning of the charade.

"Does the whole town know?" Kyle had asked in astonishment, his stomach turning over in ever tightening knots.

Douglass had laughed and said he wouldn't be surprised if it wasn't so. Most everyone in Safe Harbor had known Gracie all of her life, and she had never been a very good liar.

When Kyle asked why Douglass hadn't said anything, the reply had startled him.

"You're the first decent man she's showed interest in, Doctor," Douglass had said. "We like you, and we hoped Gracie would like you. I guess we hoped she'd finally settle her heart down, fall in love with you and make the engagement a real one."

Well, she hadn't done that, had she?

And on an unconscious level, at least, he'd been *trying* to get her to fall in love with him all summer.

And her heart had flown away to Kenya.

As he reached Lake Drive for the umpteenth time, he sighed and looked up the street, trying to decide between taking yet another turn around Market Square, or heading down the road to the hospital, to see what was going on around there.

Deciding he could be of more use at the hospital, and hoping maybe to find a way to take his mind off of Gracie for a while, he began the short walk down to the hospital, deciding he'd take advantage of the fresh air and pick up his truck later on in the day. It was only a few blocks, and it wasn't as if he couldn't use the exercise to work off some of his anxiety.

He was about halfway down Lake Drive when a familiar black Suburban came lurching down the road. It started, then stopped, then started again, screeching along as it went.

It swerved to the left, then suddenly veered right, pitching forward in front of Kyle, scratching noisily against the rough gravel as the tires met the side of the road.

Kyle ran for the Suburban with all his might, certain it was going to lurch into a ditch. He couldn't see who was driving from where he was at, but it almost had to be Wendy or Robert, and neither option was palatable to Kyle.

His stomach tight, his heart in his throat and his blood pumping with adrenaline, he ran around the back of the SUV and scrambled for the driver's side door. He slipped in the gravel and scraped his knee, but he was oblivious to the wound.

Through the tinted windows he could see Wendy slumped over the wheel, not moving.

Oh, God, take care of the baby, Kyle prayed frantically as he yanked on the door. *Take care of Wendy.*

At least the car had stopped just short of the ditch, having skidded to a hasty halt just short of the three-foot drop-off. He had that to be thankful for, as he worked frantically on the door.

The door wouldn't give, and Kyle continued to beg God for mercy. Wendy still wasn't moving, though he called her name repeatedly.

He didn't have a crowbar. He didn't have any

kind of leverage he could use to pry the door open. His mind was buzzing a million miles an hour.

He grasped for the cell phone strapped to his belt and quickly dialed 911, giving hasty directions and begging them to hurry with an ambulance and fire truck. He needed backup, and he needed it in a hurry.

In the meantime, he kept trying at the door, using his leg to give himself added leverage. He leaned back, pulling with all his weight and praying with all his might.

Suddenly, the door creaked and gave way, throwing Kyle back onto the pavement. He scraped both elbows raw and bruised the back of his shoulders, but he was completely unaware of his injuries as he scrambled to his feet and went to Wendy's aid.

She was moving a little bit now, groaning softly and attempting to open her eyes. She was scraped up and there was a lot of blood, but Kyle couldn't see any major injuries as he looked her over.

"Wendy?" Kyle called clearly, right next to her ear. He cradled her with one arm. "Wendy, it's Kyle. Can you hear me?"

"Of course I can hear you," Wendy replied stiffly, groaning again as she tried to shift her weight so she rested more comfortably against Kyle's shoulder. "You're yelling."

Kyle smiled and lowered his voice. It was just like Wendy to crack a joke in the middle of a crisis situation. He was always too straitlaced to think that way, and her humor made him laugh.

He wished Gracie were here. Her bedside manner was the best, especially in a crisis. She knew exactly how to use humor to lighten up the mood.

"What happened?" he asked in a gravelly voice, taking stock of her arms and legs, making sure nothing was sprained or broken.

"That's what I want to know," said a familiar voice, filled with warmth and sunshine, from behind Kyle's shoulder.

Gracie.

Where had she come from? He and Wendy had been alone on the road only moments before. It was as if Gracie had appeared from nowhere.

"Wendy, what in the world have you gotten yourself into this time?" Gracie kidded. "Are you planning to have this baby in the Suburban? Or are you going for some kind of odd world record we don't know about, trying to get your labor started?"

"Oooh, I'd rather not go for any world records," Wendy said, responding to the first question. "I was trying to get to the hospital just now, as a matter of fact."

"Are you in labor?" Kyle asked Wendy, realizing that might be a complication.

His mind was on Wendy's dilemma, but his heart was singing at the sight and sound of Gracie. He didn't know why she was back, and at the moment, he didn't care. He was just happy to see her here.

"I think so," Wendy conceded, running a hand along her abdomen. "This isn't like the others, though, and that's why I was rushing to the hospital. And it's why I drove off the road."

She paused as a contraction hit, then passed. Kyle noted that she looked like she was in pretty severe pain. But then, labor was like that, from what he remembered from his intern days. As a neurosurgeon, he didn't see a lot of pregnant women in labor.

"I'm having sudden, sharp pains, like someone is stabbing me with a knife," Wendy continued when she could. "They hit me suddenly, and really hard. That's why I almost drove off the road just now."

Gracie put a hand on Wendy's round stomach to feel for the strength of the contractions. "When did the pains start?" she asked softly.

"Just a little while ago."

"Who has the children?" Gracie asked softly.

"Constance is watching them. We've already made plans with her for when the baby comes."

Gracie chuckled. "Well, hon, I think that might be now."

"And Robert?" Kyle asked.

Wendy's face clenched in pain as another contraction hit her, and then shook her head. "I couldn't get him on his cell. I was trying his pager when I ran off the road."

Kyle reached for his cell phone. "Consider it done, Wendy. Don't worry about it. Robert will be there for you."

He turned and dialed, but kept one ear in the conversation behind him.

"I feel like something's wrong, Gracie. I can't explain it, I just feel it. Can you get me to the hospital soon?"

Kyle weighed his options. The ambulance would be here in a few minutes, and they were outfitted with paramedic equipment he didn't have. Wendy could be monitored on her trip to the hospital, and could be put on IV fluids right away.

Then again, time was of the essence. He could feel it in his gut. Like Wendy said—it was just a feeling. But he'd been a doctor long enough to know to follow those gut instincts.

He looked at Gracie, a question in his eyes. She immediately nodded in agreement, and reached for the back door of the Suburban.

"Scoot over, Wendy," Kyle said, gently moving her over on the front seat. "We're going to the hospital."

It didn't take more than a couple of minutes to reach the hospital, but Wendy was in bad shape, curled up and straining and sweating until her hair was damp.

Gracie had crawled up in the front seat with her in order to couch her in her arms and give her what little comfort she could. It was all she could do until they got to the hospital, but Gracie was terrified that what they were doing for Wendy was not enough.

Wendy was acting strangely. The pain had sent her inward, so that her responses became automatic and numb. The pains came more intensely and more frequently, and she would scream out in pain and call for Robert, reaching vainly for a man who was not there.

Kyle had called Robert on his cell phone. Robert was to meet them at the hospital, and was already there when they arrived.

Robert was more of a wreck than Wendy, from all outward appearances. His straight brown hair looked like it hadn't been combed for a week, and his big black eyes looked luminous in the fluorescent lights of the hospital ward.

He ran to his wife, curling his arms around her and letting her know he was there. He murmured softly, calming her with tenor of his voice.

She clung to him as they moved her from a wheelchair to a bed, where fetal monitors were immediately strapped on her and an IV inserted in her arm. It was all happening so fast, and because of the pain, Wendy was disoriented and panicky.

"Do you want something for the pain, Wendy?" Gracie asked, smoothing her sweat-soaked auburn hair back on her head and trying to sooth and calm the rattled woman. "I can give you a shot of something that will take the edge off."

Wendy shook her head vehemently. "Just get this kid out of my body," she pleaded, gritting her teeth.

"I want this labor and delivery over with. And then take care of my baby."

"We're going to do that," Kyle said, reading the charts the fetal monitor was spitting out and ignoring the fact that Wendy sounded like a drill sergeant. He noted the chart, then frowned and motioned for Gracie to follow him into the hallway.

"It's what I was afraid of," he said, his voice low and gravelly as he spoke. "The baby is in distress. We need to take the baby out right away. We need to prep Wendy for a C-section stat."

"Not a problem," Gracie said, equally grave. She knew it wasn't that easy, but there was a baby's life at stake. "I'll go let Wendy know."

She returned to the room and squeezed the hand of her patient, and her dear friend. Robert stood on the other side of the bed, his lips pressed together and his brow low, but his hand tightly laced with his wife's.

"According to the fetal monitor, your baby is experiencing distress, Wendy," Gracie said softly. "You've got to trust me that everything is going to be okay, but we are going to have to do a C-section to take your baby out right away."

"No," Wendy protested, grasping Robert's hand like a lifeline, pulling on his arm to get his support. "My other two babies were natural births."

Robert brushed the back of his fingers against Wendy's cheek. "What is important is that our precious little baby is healthy, right? That we do what we must to keep our baby safe.''

Wendy nodded miserably.

''Then we have to trust Gracie and Kyle. We have to let them make the judgment calls on the medical side of things.''

Wendy nodded again, weakly. ''I guess so. I'm scared.''

''I know,'' Gracie said, strongly squeezing Wendy's hand. ''But Robert will be with you the whole time. And so will Kyle and I. We'll be here for you. You aren't alone in this.''

Tears sprang to Wendy's eyes.

Robert spun around and strode suddenly from the room, not giving anyone the slightest idea where he was going. The anesthesiologist entered the room, and Gracie backed off with a last encouraging word to Wendy, moving into the scrub room to wash up with the other neonatal nurses and to see if she could help Robert, who was obviously struggling to accept what was happening to his wife and baby.

''I've seen this a million times,'' he was telling Kyle, who was also scrubbing up. ''But it's completely different when you're on the other side of the knife. Oh, dear Lord, it's my wife.'' He swiped a hand down his face, which looked ragged.

''Robert, you don't have to do anything today but be there to hold Wendy's hand,'' Gracie said softly. ''Today you're not a doctor, you're just a husband, here to support his wife.''

"I don't know if I can do it." He turned and punched the air.

"You can," Kyle said. "You've got to be strong for Wendy's sake. And your little baby's. Babies go into distress all the time. It might be nothing, Robert. You know that. We're only taking normal precautions here, doing what we always do in this situation."

Robert set his jaw and squared his shoulders, though tears were pouring down his cheeks. "You're right. It's just that I know what can happen. I've seen *this situation* turn out wrong. And I don't want to scare Wendy. If she looks at me—"

"If she looks at you," repeated Gracie, "she's going to see the big, strong, handsome husband she married, giving her the support she needs right now. Robert, you're about to be a daddy. For the third time. What a blessing! Now get in there and do some cheerleading for the home team."

"It's time," Kyle said, his voice velvet smooth and not showing any of the anxiety the rest of the group appeared to be feeling. "Wendy's been prepped and is being moved into surgery. Let's go welcome the newest McGuire into the world."

They rushed down the hallway and into surgery, where Wendy was lying, wide-eyed and trembling, her breath coming in short gasps through the oxygen mask on her face. A tall blue sheet stood high in the middle, separating her head from her midsection. An anesthesiologist stood by her side, monitoring her epidural and the nurses kept watch over her and her baby's vital signs.

"Robert, you need to hold Wendy's hand," Gracie instructed before moving over to assist Kyle. She hoped, for Robert's sake, that he'd decide to stay on that side of the curtain.

Kyle might be a neurologist, but when it came to emergency C-sections, he was a professional. He didn't hesitate a moment to do what needed to be done, making an incision wide enough to bring the baby's head out to where Gracie could suction the nose and mouth to get the baby breathing.

It was immediately evident what the problem was—the umbilical cord was wrapped tightly around the baby's neck, which was causing the child's drop in heartbeat and was keeping him from breathing now that he was making his entrance into the world.

Gracie slipped a glance at Kyle, who reached for her hand and gave it a quick, reassuring squeeze. She could see it in his eyes and the quick smile he slanted her—he *believed* in her.

They were a good team when they worked together. And they were going to save this baby.

She quickly clamped and cut the cord right there while it was still around the baby's neck, without moving the baby any farther, which would have caused the cord to tighten even more.

In moments, Kyle was holding a squealing infant boy up for his parents to see. The little nipper was

a bit purple, but Gracie thought he'd get over that
soon enough, as loud as he was wailing. He looked
like he was going to be a strong little boy.

"It looks like the Lord is blessing you with many
sons," Gracie said, moving forward to push the
sweat-soaked hair off Wendy's forehead and to give
her a kiss on the cheek. "We have to take this big
guy down to the nursery for a quick checkup because of the way he was born. As soon as we're
finished we'll bring him up to you so you can hold
him and feed him, okay?"

Wendy was still looking wide-eyed and astounded
at her new son. "Okay. Do what you have to do, to
make sure he's healthy. He's all right, isn't he?
There isn't a problem, is there?"

Kyle chuckled. "All right? He's got a good,
healthy kick, and a good, healthy yell. We'll give
him a thorough checkup at the nursery, but all his
outward vitals are great."

"Can I hold him for just a minute?" Wendy
begged, and Gracie could see the expression on his
face change as Kyle immediately gave in.

The old softie!

"We're supposed to rush him right off to the
nursery, but I've always believed in the sacred bond
between a mother and her child," he said softly,
almost reverently. "And I don't think a few minutes
in your arms would hurt this little guy."

He passed the baby off into Wendy's arms and

stood back, giving the family a few quiet moments with their new son.

"What's his name?" Gracie asked, stepping forward and brushing her fingers through the baby's soft, downy hair. It was auburn, like his mother's. Thick and full for a newborn, too.

"Brandon," Wendy replied, giving her son a soft kiss on the forehead, almost like a seal of his name. "Brandon Kyle."

She looked up at Kyle, smiling at his astonished expression. She nodded at him. "If that's okay with you, that is."

Kyle put a hand over his heart and nodded back. "I'm honored.

"You've got a good one, here," Wendy told Gracie, gesturing at Kyle and giving Gracie a sly wink. "Don't ever let him go."

Emotion welled up in Gracie's throat until she thought she would choke. Or burst into tears. "Don't worry. I don't intend to."

Chapter Thirteen

Gracie knew she would have to explain herself to Kyle at some point, and that the time to do so would be soon.

And she sure wasn't looking forward to that moment, either.

But that was the reason she'd returned, to make things right with Kyle. She knew she was here without knowing how the story was going to end.

At least now she knew they were still capable of working together, of serving together. It was something to draw on, at least, and she found she could take comfort in it.

Gracie took baby Brandon down to the nursery for his checkup and bath, and Kyle made sure Wendy was doing all right, giving her a complete workup to make sure the pains were gone and there was no hemorrhaging.

Neither Kyle nor Gracie would be going very far this evening, but Gracie had the feeling Kyle was going to force the issue of her leaving—and coming home—and she couldn't really blame him.

When the baby was happily back in Wendy's room and she was comfortably eating her dinner with Robert by her side to take care of little Brandon, Kyle found Gracie. He suggested they grab a hamburger from the cafeteria and find a quiet bench outside the hospital where they could eat without being disturbed.

They ate in silence for a while. Kyle seemed intent on his food, and Gracie on what she would say when he finally asked her what she had done. She kept trying to start on her own, only to fumble to a stop again when her words seemed less than adequate.

Finally, Kyle finished his burger and crumpled up the paper, tossing it into a nearby bin. He rubbed his palms on his jeans and then turned to her.

"I only want to know two things," he said around a sip of soda from a straw. "Why did you leave, and why didn't you tell me you were leaving?"

His gaze pinned her to the spot.

He looked a little bit curious, a little bit angry, a little bit disappointed.

Disappointment. That was what Gracie really couldn't handle.

"It was juvenile, okay?" she blurted, angry with herself for caring so much what he thought. "I did a stupid thing."

She paused, and he grinned, just the tip of one side of his mouth. It was charming and irritating at the same time. "No one's arguing with you."

"Oh, like you never make mistakes," she snapped back, thoroughly frustrated.

"I didn't say that," he admitted, holding up one hand. "I make mistakes. I make monumental mistakes, in fact, when you come down to it. But we're talking about *you* right now."

"Oh. Right. Limelight focused on me." She couldn't help it if she sounded a little bit sarcastic.

He just chuckled at her enthusiasm. "For the time being. I'm sure I'll get my turn. What comes around goes around."

She growled. "I sure hope so."

"Please continue." He folded his hands across his chest and cocked his head, ready to hear the whole sordid truth.

If he wanted it, he was going to get it.

"When my father made me realize that I was free to leave Safe Harbor any time I wanted, I guess I finally realized that I, of course, like an idiot, had known that all along."

She shrugged. "I suppose I was just using any available excuse to stay in town."

He raised his eyebrows.

"Why? Because I wanted to hide? Because on a subconscious level I really do want to stay in Safe Harbor and make a life here for myself? Maybe a combination of the two.

"But in being told I was free to go, I suddenly realized that I was free to stay, too."

She stopped and looked him in the eye. "*Free* to stay. And I began to think that might be what God had planned for me all along."

Kyle sighed deeply, and Gracie leveled him with a glare.

"If you tell me *I told you so* I'm going to...well, I don't know exactly what I'll do to you. But you won't like it."

He rolled his eyes dramatically and waved her on with his hand. "I'm not saying anything. Keep on with your *interesting* story."

"I went to the Women's League meeting to seek advice and guidance from them," she continued, leaning her palm into one hand and enjoying just staring at Kyle. He was handsome.

"They've all known me my whole life, practically, and I really thought they could help. Pray for me or something. I don't know."

"And couldn't they help?" He sounded genuinely curious, at least.

"I was trying to tell them about Kenya, and the missionary opportunity I had there, but they all immediately assumed I was talking about my marriage to you."

"I can definitely see the similarities," he said wryly.

"Be serious, Kyle." She sent him a scathing look to back up her words.

He looked properly repentant, though there was a

gleam of mischief in his amber eyes. Gracie wasn't sure what to think.

"I started talking about changes in my lifestyle, and they started talking about wedding showers and pastoral counseling. They were all over me with it. It was just too much."

"So you skipped town?" The humor was gone from Kyle's eyes as he spoke. "Isn't that a little overdramatic, even for you?"

Gracie sighed deeply and shook her head softly. "Kyle, when have you *ever* known me to react like an ordinary person?"

"Well, you have me there," he said, tapping his chin as if he were trying to recall something in his mind. "I can't think of a single instance."

He was still teasing her, even when he was angry with her. Hope ignited, then began to burn, slowly at first, and then with increasingly building flames within her heart.

"I just could not bear to lie to anyone anymore. Not for a single second."

She held up her hands when he would have spoken. "I know it was my idea, and it was all my doing in the first place. But it was a grievous, terrible thing to do to my friends, and I severely regret deceiving them on any issue. Even if I had good reason."

"I wouldn't worry *too* much about that," said Kyle, tongue in cheek. He looked as if he were holding back laughter.

"What's that supposed to mean?" she asked, putting up a mental shield in case she really didn't want to know, and she thought in this case she might not.

He waved her off, shaking his head as if it were not important.

"Honestly, Kyle, I was going to leave and never come back again. That was my plan. I never wanted to look any of these people in the eye again, I felt so bad about what I had done."

"But you left me holding the bag, Gracie," Kyle cut in, sounding just a little bit angry. "What was I supposed to do? You didn't tell me what you wanted. You just left."

Gracie shook her head. "I know."

"I didn't know if you wanted me to tell everyone the truth, or just keep up the masquerade of us being engaged. Either way, it wasn't fair to me. Why should I get the brunt of the blame for our deception? Your father wanted to kill me."

"You told my father?" she screeched, standing to her feet and putting a hand to her throat.

"No. I didn't tell him, Gracie. He told me. You never had that man fooled for a second. He knew exactly what you were up to. But he sure wasn't happy when you left all of the sudden."

Gracie buried her head in her hands and groaned. "Great. Now I'm really looking forward to going home tonight."

"You still haven't explained to me why you turned around and came back home. I need to know why you came home, Gracie."

"I went to Green Bay, rented a motel room and

spent a week soul searching. I walked past the mission board building a dozen times without going in. I didn't know what to do.''

"But you left in order to go to the mission field," he said, sounding confused.

"I thought I did. It's hard to let go of a childhood dream.'' She sighed loudly. "Anyway, after a week, I finally got the nerve to go into the mission board office. I had all my paperwork, and I thought I was ready to make the leap.''

"And?"

"And when I walked in the door, I had the most overwhelming sense I wasn't supposed to be there.'' She shook her head.

"I can't explain it, really. I was looking at all the exotic pictures on the walls, staring at all the faces of the people from other countries, and it was like it was all coming at me in a rush, like a freight train.

"I looked at the faces on the wall of the people in Africa, and all I could see was the faces of the little children on the dock back home. My childhood dream was staring me in the face, Kyle. I was right there, signed up and ready to go.

"And I had the sudden, overwhelming feeling the children back home were calling me, and I was not there for them.''

Kyle reached out and took her hand, squeezing it gently.

"It was as if God had thrown the gates of heaven wide-open. When I left the building, I passed a park across the street. A little boy had just been stung by a bee.

"I had my bag with me. I used my meat tenderizer, and everyone around me laughed. And all I could think of was little Joey, and Nathan, and how much I loved taking care of the people I know and love.

"People need to go and help those in Africa. But the people in Safe Harbor need help, too. And I think they need my help."

Kyle made a deep sound from his throat.

Gracie groaned again. This was absolutely miserable.

"I knew I had made a terrible mistake running away from Safe Harbor. I knew I had to go back home, as fast as I could get there. I knew I had to face my future where I belong—in Safe Harbor. And above all, I knew I had to see you again, Kyle."

"Why?" He croaked out the word, a vulnerable look on his face.

"Because."

She stopped, and he looked like he was in complete agony, so she laughed and continued.

"I needed to see your face. I needed to apologize to you for getting you into this mess in the first place. And for leaving you there when I left so suddenly."

She paused again, gathering every bit of strength and courage that was within her.

"Most of all, I had to see you again so I could tell you that I'm in love with you."

She closed her eyes and waited for the storm to hit her.

"What?"

She had muttered the last words, so it was no wonder that Kyle was reacting the way he was. He stood abruptly, moved around the picnic table, and took Gracie by the shoulders, forcing her to her feet and turning her to face him.

"What did you just say?"

Gracie cringed, but stood her ground nonetheless. She hadn't really expected this whole thing to go off well, but still...

"I said I love you," she said softly, looking up into his beautiful golden eyes. "I know it doesn't make any difference now. I know that you'll be leaving to go back to Houston soon to resume your ritzy life as a neurosurgeon...."

"Gracie," he said slowly, enunciating each word with the greatest of care. "I don't want to go back to Houston."

"You don't?" Her heart stopped beating for a full ten seconds at least.

"What's more, I don't have to go back. Robert has offered me a full partnership at the clinic if I want it."

The hope in Gracie's heart lunged swiftly up, then just as quickly took a cavernous plunge. Kyle was talking about partnerships and doctors' offices, not love and marriage.

"*Hart's Harbor,*" she said softly, "It will be a nice home for you," she said, trying to keep all the emotion from her voice. "I'm sure you'll be happy here."

His gaze narrowed on her, studying her intently. "For *us*, don't you mean?"

"Us?"

"Gracie, what am I missing here?" he said, sounding frustrated. He jammed his fingers through his thick black hair and stomped around in a circle.

Gracie shook her head. She didn't know what he was talking about.

Kyle stepped forward, framing her face in his hands. Then he leaned down and kissed her lips, tenderly and slowly.

"I think I know what it was," he said with a chuckle, caressing her cheek with his thumb. "I think I know what was missing."

He paused in his speech and smiled tenderly down at her. "I love you, Gracie Adams. Is that what you were waiting to hear?"

Hope and love roared to life in Gracie's heart. She looked up at him, questions still in her eyes.

"I will always have a special place in my heart for Melody," he said softly, stroking her cheek. "But the love I have for you is new, and real, and right, and true and strong."

She closed her eyes, then squealed and threw her arms around Kyle's neck, hugging him tightly, sure she would never let him go. "I knew it. I just knew we'd be together."

He chuckled and pulled her away from him, tucking her by his side, right where she belonged. "So, apparently, did a lot of other clever people in this remarkable little town.''

"A lot of people knew?'' she asked, looking aghast and putting a hand over her mouth.

"A lot more people than you or I imagined, I think,'' he replied smartly, with a shake of his head. "I'm guessing we didn't pull the wool over very many people's eyes.''

Gracie's mouth was wide-open in astonishment. "Then why did they let us go on like that? Why didn't they call our bluff?''

"I think, Gracie,'' Kyle said thoughtfully, "it was because they could see we were right for each other, even before we could see it for ourselves. Just think about it. We had a whole town rooting for us, Gracie. And praying for us.''

"Well, I'll be.'' Gracie let out a low, incredulous whistle. She was stunned, not just by this news but by all the events of this joyous day.

"Take this, for example,'' Kyle said, pulling a diamond ring from his pants pocket as casually as if he were pulling out a dollar bill.

"Kyle!'' Gracie exclaimed, and then cocked her hands on her hips and put on her most sassy expression. "Do you *always* carry around fancy diamond rings in your pocket, Doctor?''

He laughed. "Only on select occasions.''

Then he became serious. "Gracie, this ring belonged to Mrs. Baske's grandmother, and then her mother, and then was worn by Mrs. Baske herself. I consider it a real honor to have been given such a cherished family heirloom, and Mrs. Baske wanted me to give it to you."

"It's beautiful," she said, awe lining her voice as she looked at the ring.

"Not half as beautiful as you are tonight, Gracie Adams," Kyle said gruffly.

He slid to one knee. "Will you marry me? For real this time?"

Gracie held her hand out while Kyle slid the ring on her finger. It was a perfect fit, just as Kyle and Gracie were a perfect fit.

"For real this time," she repeated, pulling Kyle to his feet and losing herself in his cherished embrace. "Forever."

Epilogue

Kyle stood on the edge of the gazebo in the park on a block made just for the occasion. It was Labor Day, and the scene before him felt startlingly familiar.

Townsfolk filled the green, which had been set with folding chairs like a town meeting, except for the decorations everywhere that signaled *this* particular day was to be a party.

Children of all ages laughed and ran in and out between the people and chairs, waving sticks in the air like banners, or swords, or who knew what else in the imagination of the young mind. Some of the younger boys, much to their parents' chagrin, had taken to rolling down the hills in their going-to-church clothes.

Kyle spotted little Joey in the crowd, thankfully *not* waving a stick around. He was visiting just for this special day, and his mother and grandmother were hovering over them, with Nathan cheerfully nearby to keep an eye on things.

As if she sensed his gaze, Constance caught his eye and blew him a good-wishes kiss.

He laughed and shook his head. She would make him blush, right here in front of his whole town. He was feeling the heat rise to his face already, as if this penguin suit was not enough.

There was a commotion near the rear seating, and Chelsea Daniels came forward, escorted by one good-looking male and followed by another. She had more ruffles on her than a potato chip, and Kyle smiled at her typical overstatement.

She smiled back and held up her left hand, wiggling her fourth finger this way and that so Kyle was sure to catch the glint and glow of the outrageous solitaire.

His gaze slid to the poor young farmer who'd probably given up the new tractor that would have made his job easier for years in order to get her that ring. But he looked smitten, and she looked happy— at least as happy as a woman like Chelsea could be.

Kyle nodded at them and offered his silent congratulations, not caring about the satisfied gleam in Chelsea's eyes.

Kyle was still on the block, and he wanted to get this thing moving. He had places to go, literally. And as far as he was concerned, the sooner the better.

Besides, he hated standing up here like this, even for a good cause.

A moment later, music started playing, and Kyle relaxed. At least now they could get to it.

Robert escorted his wife down the middle of the aisle, in time to the music. Kyle remembered being best man at Robert's wedding, and he smiled—three boys later. Who would have thought?

Wendy stepped aside, and Robert nonchalantly slapped him on the shoulder as he passed. "Ready for this, buddy?" he asked out of the corner of his mouth.

"Ready to get on with it," Kyle quipped, deciding to keep things light. "This tuxedo is choking the life out of me."

Robert looked down the aisle and his eyes lit up. "Something tells me you won't have long to wait."

The bridal march started and everyone stood, but Kyle didn't notice. Gracie's father looked regal as he escorted her, with the bearing of something out of Irish legend in his formal kilt, but it was Gracie that caught and held Kyle's attention.

In usual, understated Gracie style, she had not gone for the super sleek, curve-fitting gowns the models wore, though she could easily have gotten away with such fashion, given her height and figure.

Likewise, she had not selected a traditional gown, one full of ruffles and lace, eyeholes and tiny buttons and bustles.

Her gown, a simple satin that reached her ankles but did not drag, shone in the sunlight. It had wide sleeves worn off the shoulder, with fabric draped across the collar. It tapered to a tiny waist and then into a full skirt.

She was lovely. No—stunning.

Kyle swept in a breath, believing he might never breathe again. She had worn her glorious red hair long. For him, because she knew that was how he liked it most.

And with every step she took toward him, toward their future, it gleamed in the sunlight. Kyle's heart was full of hope and pure, unadulterated joy.

And when he met her gaze, he saw the same emotions registered there.

No longer was he the lone man on the bachelor's block, feeling as if he was the only soul in the world. Now he was about to tie his heart and his life to Gracie and, in a very real sense, to all the people of Safe Harbor who had come out today to support them in their vows.

Vows made to God who had never left him, even when he had felt at his loneliest, and had believed in his heart that no one cared. Looking back, it was easy to see the hand of God, the many blessings in his life. It was a lesson he'd need to remember as he and Gracie embarked on their new life together as husband and wife.

He reached out his hands to her, not to take her away from her father, but rather to bind himself into this family, which he'd come to love.

Douglass gave Gracie away gladly, in his booming bass. Hand in hand, Kyle and Gracie turned forward to face the minister, and to face the exciting future God surely had for them in Safe Harbor.

* * * * *

Dear Reader,

In this story, Gracie Adams ran away from her circumstances because she couldn't see that she was making a difference in the world around her—right where she was!

Are you feeling like God has left you in the lurch? Do you feel like you are useless in the place you are right now?

I encourage you to look around you. See what kind of difference you can make in the world—right where you're at!

I hope you've enjoyed visiting the wonderful town of Safe Harbor with me. Drop me a letter and let me know what you think! I'd especially love to hear of the ways you are ministering to the world—right where you're at!

You can write me at: Deb Kastner, P.O. Box 481, Johnstown, CO 80534.

Take Care,

Deb

*Be sure to watch for
the heartwarming conclusion to the
SAFE HARBOR miniseries,
coming next month to Love Inspired.
And now for a sneak preview of
HOME TO SAFE HARBOR,
please turn the page*

Chapter One

Reverend Justine Clemens stood frozen before the entire congregation of First Peninsula Church, managing to hold a smile in place through sheer determination. In her hands, she held the plaque she'd just accepted amid thunderous applause. Clearly, everyone thought she should be thrilled.

They were certainly thrilled.

But she was devastated.

The sign on her new office door would not read Reverend Justine Clemens—Assistant Pastor. That's what she'd thought Reverend Burns and the board meant when they'd asked her to stay on permanently to assist him. But instead the plaque she now held tightly clutched in her hands read Reverend Justine Clemens—Women and Youth Pastor.

Once again she'd been relegated to a traditional role for women in the church. Once again she was on the road to having no one and nothing to call her own.

When Reverend Burns retired—and at seventy how far off could that be?—she'd thought these people would be her flock. That they would look to her for guidance. Be her family.

The corners of the brass plaque bit into her hands and she managed to relax her trembling grip just a little. But, as she did, she also had to blink back the tears that threatened to give her away. Reverend Burns had just handed her what he clearly thought of as first prize but she knew it to be the honorable mention it was.

He stood next to her at the reception following the service, smiling and looking more like a man of sixty these days.

"You're upset," Reverend Burns said when there was a break in the line of parishioners who'd come over to congratulate her on her new role. His brows were drawn together in a worried frown.

Justine started and felt a blush heat her face. If he knew did everyone know?

"Relax. I doubt anyone else noticed but I know you too well to be fooled by that pasted-on smile. What is it, dear?"

Justine had never been able to hide the truth from Reverend Burns, not from that first day he'd caught her cutting school and enjoying a cigarette behind the gazebo in Safe Harbor Park with her new friends.

"I thought you asked me to stay on to be your assistant.

"That's exactly what you will be."

Justine turned the plaque she still held toward him. "But it's a ministry limited to women and children."

The older man sighed, shaking his head slightly. "You're still seeing the glass half-empty, Justine. You are an absolute wonder with the teens and younger women, not to mention the little ones. You relate to them in a way I find I no longer can. They make up a good portion of the congregation. I want them going to you for help. You can do a lot of good."

She felt her face heat, embarrassed by what sounded like selfish motives. The words tumbled out. "I thought I was being put in position to take your place one day. And I know you and the board wouldn't have limited the scope of my ministry if you had confidence in me that I could replace you."

"But we do have confidence in you," Reverend Burns said gently. "You must seek God's plan for your life, dear, not your own. I very much fear that is what you've been doing all along." He held up his hand to stop her automatic defense. "I'm not saying your call to the ministry wasn't real. I'm saying that maybe He has something for you that you're blind to. I don't know what His plan is, but for now why not do the job He's sent you and see what comes of it?"

Justine nodded jerkily, trying to hold back the

emotions that surged in her. She could see the wisdom in his words, but following his advice would be a struggle.

"Excuse me, Reverend Clemens. Reverend Burns." A deep voice interrupted her struggle for composure. "I wonder if I might have a word with you before the kids descend on us."

Past hurts and new ones flew out of Justine's mind when she followed the sound of that husky voice to a point just over her head.

It was *him*.

At five foot ten she wasn't used to looking up at many people. At least not as far as she had to look up right now. She found herself snared by eyes even a deeper brown than her own. They were nearly obsidian. A rich dark chocolate.

For weeks she'd seen Matthew Trent around town and in church and now she had a voice to put with that hauntingly handsome face. A dangerous combination of tall, dark and gorgeous, he was the new chief of police and he distracted Justine every time she noticed him. Once, even in the middle of a sermon!

No man had ever affected her the way he did. No man had ever taken her eyes off her ministry or made her heart pump harder with the sound of his voice. There were times she wished she had the courage to take a chance on love and a family but those things were not for her. She couldn't be a pastor *and* a mother. Leading a church was too demanding. It wouldn't be fair to the children. And besides that, she couldn't be a mother without first being a wife and she'd never trust any man with her heart. She'd watched firsthand what could happen to a woman who loved and lost. Especially when the man appeared to be all that was brave, heroic and trustworthy.

Take 2 inspirational love stories FREE!

PLUS get a FREE surprise gift!

Mail to Steeple Hill Reader Service™

In U.S.
3010 Walden Ave.
P.O. Box 1867
Buffalo, NY 14240-1867

In Canada
P.O. Box 609
Fort Erie, Ontario
L2A 5X3

YES! Please send me 2 free Love Inspired® novels and my free surprise gift. After receiving them, if I don't wish to receive anymore, I can return the shipping statement marked cancel. If I don't cancel, I will receive 3 brand-new novels every month, before they're available in stores! Bill me at the low price of $3.99 each in the U.S. and $4.49 each in Canada, plus 25¢ shipping and handling and applicable sales tax, if any*. That's the complete price and a saving of over 10% off the cover prices—quite a bargain! I understand that accepting the books and gift places me under no obligation ever to buy any books. I can always return a shipment and cancel at any time. Even if I never buy another book from Steeple Hill, the 2 free books and the surprise gift are mine to keep forever.

103 IDN DNU6
303 IDN DNU7

Name	(PLEASE PRINT)
Address	Apt. No.
City	State/Prov. Zip/Postal Code

Love Inspired

HOME TO
SAFE HARBOR

BY

KATE WELSH

Determined to prove herself, Reverend Justine Clemens returned to the town where she'd spent her troubled youth. Resigned to living her life alone, she poured all her hopes and dreams into her new ministry. But God clearly had other plans for this as He brought her head-to-head with Chief Matthew Trent. Would Justine finally take a chance on love?

Don't miss
HOME TO SAFE HARBOR
the final installment of
SAFE HARBOR
The town where everyone finds shelter from the storm!

On sale June 2003
Available at your favorite retail outlet.